Ever since **Lisa Childs** read her first romance novel (a Mills & Boon story, of course) at age eleven, all she wanted was to be a romance writer. With over forty novels published with Mills & Boon, Lisa is living her dream. She is an award-winning, bestselling romance author. Lisa loves to hear from readers, who can contact her on Facebook, through her website, www.lisachilds.com, or her snail-mail address, PO Box 139, Marne, MI 49435, USA.

**Also by Lisa Childs**

Discover more at millsandboon.co.uk

# COLTON'S CINDERELLA BRIDE

### LISA CHILDS

MIX
Paper from
responsible sources
FSC
FSC C007454

This book is produced from independently certified FSC™
paper to ensure responsible forest management.

For more information visit: www.harpercollins.co.uk/green

Printed and bound in Spain
by CPI, Barcelona

## MILLS & BOON

First Published in Great Britain 2018
by Mills & Boon, an imprint of HarperCollins*Publishers*
1 London Bridge Street, London, SE1 9GF

*Colton's Cinderella Bride* © 2018 Harlequin Books S.A.

Special thanks and acknowledgement are given to Lisa Childs for her contribution to *The Coltons of Red Ridge* series.

ISBN: 978-0-263-26584-2

With great appreciation for my amazing family—my immediate family and to all my aunts, uncles and cousins who support me, too! I am so fortunate to have you all in my life!

# Chapter 1

*Everything happens for a reason...*

Mama had told Juliette that so many times over the years and so often during the long months of her terminal illness. Not wanting to argue with or upset an invalid, Juliette had just nodded as if she'd agreed with her. But she hadn't really. She had seen no reason for Mama getting sick and dying, no reason to work two jobs to pay off Mama's medical bills and her own community college tuition.

But as she stared up at the little blond-haired angel sitting atop the playground slide, her heart swelled with love, and she knew Mama had been right. Everything happens for a reason, and Pandora was that reason.

Her daughter was Juliette's reason for everything

that had happened in the past and for everything that she did in the present.

"Is it too high?" she called up to the little girl who'd convinced Juliette that since turning four, she was old enough to go down the big kid slide. She was small for her age, though, and looked so tiny sitting up so high that a twinge of panic struck Juliette's heart.

Maybe she was just uneasy because it looked as though it might start storming at any moment. The afternoon sky had turned dark, making it look more like dusk than five thirty. Since July in Red Ridge, South Dakota, was usually hot and dry, rain would be a welcome relief—as long as it came without lightning and thunder, which always scared Pandora.

Juliette probably shouldn't have stopped at the park that apparently everyone else had deserted for fear of the impending storm. But when she'd finished her shift as a Red Ridge K9 officer, and had picked up her daughter from day care, the little girl had been so excited to try the slide that she hadn't been able to refuse.

"Come on, honey," she encouraged Pandora as she pushed back a strand of her own blond hair that had slipped free of her ponytail. "I'm right here. I'll catch you when you reach the bottom." She wouldn't let her fall onto the wood chips at the foot of the slide.

"I'm not scared, Mommy," Pandora assured her. "It's supercool up here. I can see all around…" She trailed off as she stared into the distance. Maybe she could see the storm moving in on them.

As if she sensed it, too, Sasha—Juliette's K9 partner—leaped up from the grass on which she'd been snoozing.

Her nose in the air, the beagle strained against her leash that Juliette had tethered around a light pole. Sniffing the air, she emitted a low growl.

Despite the heat, a chill passed through Juliette. Sasha had been trained for narcotics detection. But what was she detecting and from where? Nobody else was in the park right now. Maybe the scent of drugs had carried on the wind from someplace else, someplace nearby.

"Mommy!" Pandora called out, drawing Juliette's attention back to where she was now half standing, precariously, at the top of the slide.

"Honey, sit down," Juliette said, her heart thumping hard with fear.

Pandora ignored her as she pointed across the park. "Why did that man shoot that lady with the purple hair?"

Juliette gasped. "What?"

Pandora pointed again, and her tiny hand shook. "Over there, Mommy. The lady fell down in the parking lot and she's not getting back up."

Like her daughter, Juliette was quite small, so she couldn't see beyond the trees and playground equipment to where her daughter gestured. She hurried toward the slide and vaulted up the steps to the top. Then she looked in the direction Pandora was staring, and she sucked in a sharp breath. About two hundred feet away, in the parking lot behind the playground area, a woman lay on the ground, a red stain spreading across her white shirt while something red pooled on the asphalt beneath her.

"Oh, no…" Juliette murmured. She needed to get

to the woman, needed to get her help…but before she could reach for her cell to call for it, a car door slammed and an engine revved. That car headed over the grass, coming across the playground.

The shooter must have noticed Pandora watching him and figured she'd witnessed him shooting—maybe killing—someone.

Juliette's heart pounded as fear overwhelmed her. She wrapped her arms around Pandora and propelled them both down the slide. Ordinarily her daughter would have squealed in glee, but now she trembled with the same fear that gripped Juliette.

The car's engine revved again as it jumped the curb and careened toward them. Juliette drew her gun from her holster as she gently pushed Pandora into the tunnel beneath the slide. The side of the thick plastic tunnel faced the car, which had braked to an abrupt stop. A door creaked open.

Juliette raised her finger to her lips, gesturing at Pandora to stay quiet. The little girl stared up at her, her green eyes wide with fear. But she nodded.

Sasha was not quiet. She barked and growled, straining against her leash. Instinctively she knew Juliette and Pandora were in danger. But with the man between them now, Juliette could not release her partner to help. And maybe that was a good thing. She had no doubt that Sasha would put her life in danger for Juliette's and especially for Pandora's.

Juliette would put herself in danger for Pandora, too.

Crouched on the other side of the tunnel so he wouldn't see her, Juliette studied the man who'd stepped out of the sedan. He'd pulled the hood of his light jacket up over his head, and despite the overcast sky, he wore sunglasses. He was trying hard to disguise himself. But was it already too late? Had Pandora seen him without the hood and the glasses?

Who was he?

A killer.

She had no doubt that the young woman he'd shot was bleeding out in the parking lot. Frustration and guilt churned inside her, but she couldn't call for help now and alert him to where she'd hidden her daughter. If not for Pandora, the cop part of Juliette would have been trying to take him down—even without backup. But because Pandora was in danger, the mother part of her overruled the cop.

Especially since he was heading straight toward the slide. But Pandora was no longer perched atop it. So he looked around, and he tensed as he noticed the tunnel beneath it. He raised his gun, pointing the long barrel toward that tunnel.

Toward Juliette's daughter...

Her heart pounding so hard it felt as if it might burst out of her chest, she raised her gun and shouted, "Police. Drop your weapon! You're under arrest!"

Instead he swung the gun toward her, and his glasses slid down his nose, revealing eyes so dark and so cold that a shiver passed through Juliette.

He shook his head and yelled, "Give me the damn kid!"

And she knew—Pandora had seen him without the hat, without the glasses. Then the wind kicked up again and blew his hood back, and Juliette saw his dark curly hair. And something pinged in her mind. He looked familiar to her, but she wasn't sure where she'd seen him before.

"Put down the gun!" she yelled back at him.

But he moved his finger toward his trigger, so she squeezed hers. When the bullet struck his shoulder, his face contorted into a grimace of pain. He cursed— loudly.

"Stop!" she yelled. "Drop the gun!"

Despite his wounded shoulder, he held tightly to his weapon. Before she could fire again, he turned and ran back toward his car. Over his shoulder, he called out, "That kid is dead and so are you, lady cop!"

Juliette started after him. But a scream drew her attention. And a little voice called out urgently, "Mommy!"

The car peeled out of the lot, tires squealing against the asphalt. Juliette stared after it, trying to read the license plate number, but it was smeared with mud. From where? The weather here had been so dry.

He'd planned to obscure that plate. He'd planned to kill that woman.

Now he planned to kill her and Pandora. She moved toward the end of the tunnel and leaned over to peer inside at her daughter. "Sweetheart, are you okay?"

The little girl's head bobbed up and down in a jerky nod. "Are you dead, Mommy?"

A twinge struck Juliette's heart. "No, I'm fine, honey." But that woman was not. She pulled out her cell phone and punched 911. After identifying herself as a police officer, she ordered an ambulance for the shooting victim, an APB on the killer's car and her K9 team to help.

But she knew they would arrive too late. She doubted that woman could be saved, and she was worried that the killer might not be caught. At least not until he killed again...

And he'd made it clear who his next targets would be. Her and her daughter...

Pandora began to cry, her soft voice rising and cracking with hysteria as her tiny body shook inside the tunnel. Juliette's legs began to shake, too, then gave out so that she dropped to her knees. She crawled inside the small space with her daughter and pulled her tightly into her arms.

Pandora was Juliette's life. She could not lose her. She had to do whatever necessary to protect her.

*What the hell am I doing back here?*

There was nothing in Red Ridge for Blake Colton. He'd built his life in London and Hong Kong and Singapore— because his life was his business. And those were the cities in which he'd built Blake Colton International into the multibillion-dollar operation that it was.

That was undoubtedly why Patience had called him—because of his money—since he and his sister had never been close. He wasn't close to any of his other sisters, either, or to his father or mother. Maybe that was partially his fault, though, because he'd left home so young and had been gone so long now. But Patience hadn't called to see how he was doing; she'd called to ask him to help.

He didn't know how he could provide the kind of help his family needed, though. In addition to their father's business problems, she'd told him about a murderer on the loose. A murderer everyone believed to be a Colton, too—one of Blake's cousins.

Blake pulled his rental vehicle into an empty parking spot outside the long one-story brick building on Main Street—the Red Ridge Police Department. Maybe his cousin Finn, who was the police chief, could explain to him just what the hell was really going on in Red Ridge.

But only Blake could answer the question of what had compelled him to hop on his private plane and head back to Red Ridge. And he had no damn idea...

With a sigh, he pushed open the driver's door and stepped out. The sky was dark with the threat of a storm that hadn't come. Blake felt the weight of those clouds hanging over him like guilt.

He knew what Patience wanted—what she expected him to do. Bail out their father so that their sister Layla wasn't forced to marry some old billionaire to save Colton Energy. How like their father to care more about his company than his kids...

That was the Fenwick Colton whom Blake knew and had spent most of his life resenting. But he could understand his father a little better now. Blake didn't have any kids, but his company was like his child. If he withdrew the kind of money required to save Colton Energy, he could cripple his own business and put thousands out of work.

He couldn't do that—not for his father and not even for Layla. There had to be another way. Finn probably wouldn't have any answers to that, but he would know all there was to know about this crazy "Groom Killer" targeting men about to be married. At least the threat of dying had caused Layla's fiancé to end their engagement. But according to Patience, that threat was hurting her sister Beatrix's bridal shop business. It was also affecting their youngest sister Gemma's personal life because her boyfriend would not get as serious with her as she would have liked.

With a rumble of thunder sounding ominously in the distance, Blake hurried toward the doors of the police department. He didn't want to get caught in a deluge. A woman rushed toward the building, as well. She had one arm wrapped around a child on her hip and the other hand holding the leash of the beagle running ahead of her. He stepped forward and reached around her to open the door, and as he did, he caught a familiar scent.

He hadn't smelled it in years. Nearly five years…

But he'd never forgotten the sweet fragrance and the woman who'd worn it. It hadn't been perfume, though. She'd said it had been her shampoo, so it had been light, smelling like rain and honeysuckle.

The scent wafted from the woman, whose pale shade of long hair was the same as the woman who'd haunted him the past five years. But it couldn't be her…

He'd looked for her—after that night—and hadn't been able to find her anywhere. She must have checked out of the hotel and left town.

She certainly hadn't been a Red Ridge police officer

like this woman. She wore the distinctive uniform of a K9 cop and held the leash of her partner. But when she turned back toward him, her gaze caught his and held. And he recognized those beautiful blue eyes...

Remembered her staring up at him as he'd lowered his head to kiss her...

But no, it could not be her. Being back in Red Ridge, staying at the Colton Plaza Hotel, had brought up so many memories of her, of that night, that he was starting to imagine her everywhere.

He'd found her easily enough. But he couldn't take out her or her daughter here—outside the damn Red Ridge Police Department. Hell, after that bitch had shot him, he could barely raise his arm.

Blood trickled yet from the wound, soaking into his already saturated sleeve. He needed medical attention. But he'd have to find it somewhere other than a hospital or doctor's office. RRPD would have someone watching those places, waiting for him.

Damn the timing...

The park had looked deserted. He hadn't noticed anyone else around—until he'd heard the dog bark. Then he'd seen the little girl—but not before she had watched him fire those shots into that thieving dealer's chest. Did she understand what she'd witnessed?

She was old enough that she probably did. And because he hadn't known anyone else was around, he hadn't had his hood up or glasses on then. So she would be able to identify and testify against him. And so would her damn cop mama.

But that wasn't going to happen.

She and her mother were not going to live long enough to bring him down.

# Chapter 2

*Noooo...*

Not now. Not ever...

Juliette had determined long ago that she would never see Blake Colton again. Even though she had heard that he'd recently returned to Red Ridge, she hadn't thought that she would actually run into him. It wasn't as if she worked at the Colton Plaza Hotel anymore.

And she hadn't expected him to show up at the Red Ridge Police Department.

What was he doing here—now?

She froze as their gazes locked. She should have been running instead—running away from *him* with Pandora. But she hesitated too long before stepping through that door. And his gaze went from her face to her daughter's.

While there was no mistaking that Pandora was her biological child, the little girl's blond hair was darker than Juliette's—more a dark gold like Blake's. Pandora's eyes were green instead of blue. Green like her father's eyes that stared at her now, widening with shock. She also had the same dimple in her left cheek that he had, but since neither was smiling now, it was just a small dimple and not the deep dent it became when they grinned.

Pandora wasn't grinning, though. She was sobbing; she hadn't stopped since the man had come after them despite Juliette's assurances that they were safe now. Juliette didn't feel safe, though.

Pandora must not have, either, because she buried her face in Juliette's neck, hiding from the handsome stranger who held the door for them. But she'd done that too late. He'd already seen the little girl just like he'd seen Juliette.

And from the expression crossing his handsome face, Juliette could tell that he'd recognized her despite the nearly five years that had passed. From the way he was staring at Pandora, with his brow furrowed as if he was doing math in his head, he might have also realized that the child in her arms could be his.

No. They were not safe.

He turned back to Juliette, and the look in his green eyes chilled her nearly as much as the look in the killer's dark eyes had. She shivered.

"It's you—" he murmured "—isn't it?"

She shook her head in denial. "I—I don't know what you're talking about…"

His eyes narrowed with skepticism and suspicion. "It is you. And she…" He raised his hand as if to reach for Pandora.

But Juliette spun around, keeping her child away from him. "She's just witnessed a crime," she said, her voice cracking with regret and fear that her poor little girl had had to see what she had. A murder…

"I can't do this now," she told him. But before she could rush through those doors and get away from him, someone rushed out.

Like Juliette, the woman was clad in a RRPD uniform, her brown eyes dark with concern.

"Oh, my God," Elle Gage exclaimed. "I just heard what happened. Are you all right?" She focused on the little girl. "Is Pandora?"

"Pandora…" Blake murmured the name, drawing Elle's attention to him.

She gasped. "You—you're Blake Colton," she said. Then she glanced at Juliette. She was the only one who knew—the only one Juliette had trusted with the truth. "Were you at the park, too?" she asked him.

Blake's brow furrowed. "Park?" He turned toward Juliette. "Is that where the crime happened?"

She nodded. "I need to complete the report." But that wasn't all she wanted to do. She wanted to make sure she had a safe place for her daughter. Pandora needed protection from at least one man—the one who'd sworn she would die. She might need protecting from this one, too, if he had realized that he was Pandora's father.

"But I need to talk to you," he said through teeth gritted with frustration and anger.

Elle reached for Pandora, extricating the little girl from Juliette's arms. "Come here, sweetheart," she said. "Let you, me, and Sasha get something to eat and drink…" She took the beagle's leash from Juliette's hand, too, and with a crook of her neck gestured at Blake. Since she'd learned he'd returned to town a couple of days ago, she'd been urging Juliette to talk to him.

But there really was no time. Not now…

Fear pounded in her heart as she watched her friend walk away with her daughter. She'd nearly lost her just a short time ago—at the park. If Juliette hadn't shot the man in the shoulder…

If she hadn't wounded him, he would have killed them both. She just had to convince her boss of the same. She had no time to deal with Blake Colton. But when she moved to follow Elle and Pandora, he caught her. Wrapping his big hand around her arm, he held her back.

Her skin tingled from his touch. It had been so long. But she could still remember how it felt…how he'd touched her that night…

She jerked her arm from his grasp. Just as he'd spoken through gritted teeth, she did the same. "I. Cannot. Do. This. Now."

"We need to talk," he insisted.

She knew it was true and not just because Elle had been badgering her to seek him out. She knew it was the right thing to do. But at the moment she needed to be with her daughter—needed to see for herself that her child stayed safe.

"She's mine, isn't she?" he asked, and his voice cracked slightly with the emotions making his green eyes dark.

Her reply stuck in her throat, choking her.

"She's the right age," he continued as if he was trying to convince himself. "And she looks like me…"

Juliette felt like she had when she'd stared into the barrel of the killer's gun. Trapped. Terrified. Desperate…

Frustration gripped Blake, twisting his gut into tight knots. He wanted to shake her, but when he reached for her again, she flinched as if she expected him to hurt her. He wouldn't have, of course—despite his feelings. But he dropped his hand back to his side.

"Tell me," he said, badgering her like she was a reluctant witness on the stand. "Tell me if she's mine."

"Yes!" she exclaimed, as if her patience had snapped. Or perhaps it was her conscience. "She's yours."

He expelled a sharp breath, like she'd punched him in the gut. All these years he'd spent thinking about her and about that night, he had never once considered that she might have gotten pregnant—that they might have made a child together. He was a father.

Anger coursed through him now, replacing the shock. "How—how could…"

Her lips curved into a slight smile. "The usual way…"

He glared at her. "How could you keep her from me?"

Her face flushed now, but she just stared at him with those damn beautiful eyes of hers.

"How could you?" he asked. "For years?"

"I—I—" she stammered. "You left Red Ridge right after…"

"You could have found me," he insisted. His family was in Red Ridge. They'd known where he was.

She tensed now and glared back at him. "You could have found me—even without knowing."

"I tried," he admitted. "You slipped out in the middle of the night, and I didn't even know your last name. Hell, right now I'm not sure you gave me your right first name, *Juliette*."

She flinched.

And he wondered. Had she told him anything that was the truth?

"Juliette is my real name," she said.

Someone from inside the police department called it now. She glanced back toward the building. "I—I need to go," she said. But when she started forward, he caught her arm again—stopping her.

"No—" He'd spent five years wondering what had happened to her. Where she was… He wasn't just going to let her walk away from him again.

"She needs me," Juliette said.

And he felt once again like she'd struck him. The child needed her *mother*. She didn't even know she had a *father*. Unless Juliette had passed off another man as the little girl's daddy. Blake glanced down at the hand of the arm he held—her left hand. Her fingers were bare of any rings. She wasn't married or engaged now.

But a lot could have happened over the last nearly five years. She might have had a husband. Hell, he'd thought she might have on their night together, and that was why she'd slipped away like she had, so nobody would spot them together.

She hadn't worn a ring then either, though. So maybe, as a cop, she'd just decided not to wear one.

How had she afforded that beautiful gown—those shoes and earrings—on a cop's salary—if she'd even been a cop back then? She looked younger now, without makeup, than she'd looked that night.

"Let me go," she said—once again through gritted teeth. She had beautiful teeth and lips and features...

He'd started to believe that he'd romanticized her and that night over the years. That she couldn't have been nearly as beautiful as he'd thought she was. He'd been wrong—about romanticizing it.

She was also stressed and afraid, her face pale and eyes wide with fear.

"I will let you go," he agreed because he had no choice. Her daughter—*their* daughter—needed her.

Before the little girl had hidden her face in her mother's neck, Blake had noticed her tears and, worse than that, her fear. His gut churned again—with a sense of helplessness even worse than when Patience had told him about his sister Layla's predicament.

"But you're going to come to my suite later," he told her.

Her eyes narrowed as if she thought he expected a

repeat of that long-ago night. Of what had happened over and over that night…

His pulse leaped at the thought, but he was too angry with her to ever want her again. So he clarified, "Just to talk."

Someone called her name a second time, and she tugged free of him. But as she stepped through those open doors to the lobby, she turned back and nodded.

"I'm staying in the same suite as I was that night," he told her.

Color rushed back into her pale face, and she nodded again. She would be there. Eventually. But he suspected it might be a while before she could make it.

Still reeling from what he'd just learned, he no longer wanted to talk to his cousin—the police chief. Blake didn't want to step into that police department where she and their daughter were.

He just wanted to be alone. He wanted to think and process and deal with all the emotions gripping him. The anger, the shock, the fear…

His daughter had witnessed a crime of some sort, and from the way both she and her mother had acted, they were definitely frightened.

Could they be in danger? Could he lose his child just as he had finally discovered her existence?

"He's back?" Fenwick Colton already knew that his son had returned to Red Ridge. The concierge at the Colton Plaza Hotel had confirmed that Blake had checked into a suite on the twenty-first floor a couple of days ago. But Fenwick hadn't seen him. And he sure as hell hadn't heard from him.

Patience, Fenwick's daughter and Blake's half sister, nodded in reply, but she had to understand what he was really asking. Why hadn't Blake come to see him?

The boy was Fenwick's only son. They should have been close. Fenwick had had primary custody of him, since a hyper boy had been more than his jet-setting mother had wanted to handle. But the kid had always acted like he couldn't stand to be near him. And as if to prove it, he'd spent the past five years living in other countries. Maybe that was just because he was like his mother, though.

"Why is he back?" Fenwick asked his daughter.

Patience lowered her head slightly, and her dark bangs shielded her dark eyes. She was staring down at her desk in her office at the Red Ridge K9 training center. If he wanted to talk to his daughter, he usually had to come to the training center, where she worked as a veterinarian. It was the same with Bea; he would have had to go to the bridal shop to see her. At least Gemma visited him, but it was usually to ask for money.

He ran his hands over his tailored suit, plucking a strand of dog hair from the expensive fabric. Then he touched his hair, making sure the blond piece hadn't slipped. As mayor of Red Ridge, he had to make sure he always looked good. "You called him," he surmised.

"I had to," she said, and her voice was sharp with resentment. Patience didn't understand business like Layla did. Like Blake did…

"He's not going to help," Fenwick said. It wasn't a

question. He knew that with just as much certainty as he knew that Blake had returned to Red Ridge.

Patience looked up from her desk now. "He might. He will," she persisted, but she sounded more like she was trying to convince herself than she was him. "Why else did he come home?"

That was what worried Fenwick. If Blake hadn't come back to help his family, then he probably had another reason—a personal reason—for returning to Red Ridge.

"You shouldn't have called him," Fenwick admonished her.

"He's your son," she said. "My brother. He deserved to hear what's going on with the family from one of us."

Fenwick suspected the media had probably beaten Patience to the punch, though. Coltons were news. And a Colton scandal was even bigger news.

Damn his reprobate cousin Rusty and his equally disreputable kids for causing such a scandal. But it went beyond a scandal. Rusty's daughter Demi was a murderer. Evidence and witnesses proved—to him, at least—that she was the psycho killing grooms-to-be because she'd been dumped by her own one-week fiancé. Of course a Colton being a killer wasn't news. Other Colton family members—very distant family members out of state—had committed murder, as well.

Fenwick didn't know what he might be forced to do if Layla wasn't able to carry out their plan of marrying to save the company. This damn Groom Killer nonsense was threatening their livelihood. But now that might not be all that was threatened.

"You shouldn't have called him," Fenwick repeated, "because you might have put him in danger."

Patience's dark eyes narrowed. "What are you talking about?"

"This maniac," Fenwick said, "is killing grooms. *Men*." He was a little scared for himself—not that he had any intention of getting married again. Three times was more than enough. And he had more fun dating than he'd ever had being married.

"Blake isn't engaged," Patience said. "He's not marrying anyone. He didn't even have a serious girlfriend when he did live at home. So I doubt there's anyone in Red Ridge he would be tempted to propose to."

Fenwick wished he could trust that. "Couples are afraid to go public. Engagements have been canceled. Everyone is afraid of the Groom Killer. But that hasn't stopped anyone from coupling up in private."

He could think of at least six new couples in Red Ridge—some damn unlikely couples.

"And you know your brother," Fenwick continued. "If anyone tells that stubborn kid not to do something, he's twice as determined to do it."

Like build his own damn company. Fenwick had told the boy not to do it, that he didn't have what it took. Hell, he'd been fresh out of graduate school with his MBA and had no real business experience when he'd begun his "start-up." But Blake had had to go out and prove him wrong.

He was so damn stubborn it would be just like him

to try to prove Fenwick wrong now about getting engaged. But then he wouldn't be risking just some money. He would be risking his life.

# Chapter 3

Juliette sat on one of the chairs in the row outside the chief's office. She'd given her report and she had helped Pandora give hers as well as a description of the shooter to Detective Carson Gage who would be working the murder case.

The last thing the Red Ridge Police Department could handle right now was another murder investigation. They were already spread so thin with the Groom Killer murders and the suspected criminal activities of the Larson twins. Did the RRPD have enough resources left to protect Pandora? That was what Juliette wanted to know, what she waited outside the chief's office to discuss with him.

But of course, Finn Colton was busy. So busy that she had to wait. The receptionist was busy, as well, taking one call after another. Usually they would have had time to talk while Juliette waited to see the chief. She would have asked Lorelei about her teenage kids, and Lorelei would have asked about Pandora.

Elle was with Pandora, coloring pictures in the conference room and trying to get her to eat the pizza she'd ordered for them. Elle was a good friend.

The only person Juliette had told about that night nearly five years ago. The night she'd felt like Cinderella being invited to the ball.

The invitation she'd received had come in the form of a tip from a hotel guest. Juliette had been cleaning the woman's room all week. She'd sought Juliette out a couple of times for more towels, to restock the minibar, and she'd talked to her like Juliette was a person and not just a maid. The woman had compelled Juliette to confide in her about working two jobs to pay off her late mother's medical bills and tuition for community college.

So later that week Juliette was disappointed that the woman had checked out before her business conference ended. She was even more surprised that instead of finding money as a tip, she found a note lying atop a glittering mound of a gown and some sky-high heels and long, dangling glittery earrings. The note read:

No cash for a tip, but take these as thanks. Had my heart broken in them and will never wear again.

Juliette wasn't so sure that was the case. The woman she'd met had seemed too strong and self-reliant to care much if her heart had been broken. She'd probably left her the items instead of cash because she'd known the cash would have just gone toward those medical bills. The shoes and earrings and that glittery gown were something Juliette never would have bought for herself. One, she couldn't have afforded them. And two, she wouldn't have needed them since she had no place to wear them. But lying beneath the note was a ticket granting her entry to the conference awards black tie dinner.

Because of her mom's long illness, Juliette had skipped her high school prom a couple of years ago. It hadn't mattered much to her then—not as much as it had meant to her mother, who'd felt so bad that Juliette hadn't attended it. But it wasn't as if Juliette had had a date anyway. And even if she had, she wouldn't have wanted to miss a minute left of her mother's limited time.

Juliette had already forgotten her father because he had died when she was very young. At least now her parents, who'd been high school sweethearts, were together again.

And Juliette was alone. Should she dress up and give herself the prom she'd missed? But instead of goofing around with high school kids who didn't understand how precious life was, she would be socializing with adults, with accomplished businesspeople.

The idea thrilled her too much for her to resist. The guest had been like a fairy godmother leaving behind that dress and heels and earrings. All that was missing were the carriage and the horses. But Juliette didn't need a pumpkin and some mice. She had her own vehicle.

When her shift ended, she left the hotel in her maid's drab uniform with her *tips* tucked inside her backpack. Her friend, who was going to cosmetology school, was thrilled to do her hair and makeup, so just a few short hours later, Juliette returned to the hotel where she worked. But not even her coworkers recognized her as she swept into the ballroom wearing those impossibly high and dainty heels as well as the long, nude-colored glittery gown. Her hair was half up and half down in some complicated style that defied gravity. And when she moved, the long dangling earrings brushed against her neck. For the first time in her life, Juliette felt like a princess. Even then she'd suspected it would be the last time she would ever feel like this.

So she'd vowed then and there to make the most of this magical evening. To experience everything that she could—because she knew very well how short life could be. Her *ball* wasn't exactly what she'd expected, though. Her fairy godmother must not have been the only one who'd cut the conference short, because the ballroom was not crowded, which made *him* impossible to miss.

He was younger than most of the other men in the room, and by far the most handsome in his black tuxedo. He was lean and muscular and just the right height that with these heels on, she would be able to stare into his eyes. Eyes that she knew were green and sharp with his keen intelligence. He wasn't much older than she was, but he already had his MBA.

Blake Colton. The only male heir of the wealthy

branch of the Colton family. He was the prince of Red Ridge. And Juliette was…

For the night, Cinderella.

She felt the moment he noticed her—because her pulse quickened, and her skin began to tingle. She didn't even need to look up to know that he was coming toward her. Her heart beat faster and faster as he drew nearer to her.

"Hello," a deep voice murmured.

She turned and stared right into his eyes. And she knew in that moment, she never wanted to look away. She didn't just see him; she saw herself in his eyes—the way she wanted to be: beautiful, interesting, happy.

He sucked in a breath, and she knew that he felt it, too—that instant and intense attraction between them. He extended a hand to her, and it shook slightly. "I—I'm Blake Colton."

She knew who he was. Hell, everybody in Red Ridge knew who he was. But he didn't know that she was from Red Ridge. She could have been from anywhere—could have been anyone. And for tonight, she could pretend that she was.

But her first instinct was to be honest, so she murmured, "I'm Juliette…" And she put her hand in his.

He cocked his head, and a lock of dark blond hair tumbled across his forehead. He was obviously waiting for her last name.

But instead of giving it to him, she just smiled.

He chuckled. "You're going to be mysterious," he said.

Her smile widened. "I'm going to be smart."

Just in case she got caught crashing the event, she

didn't want to get fired from her job. Technically, since he was a Colton, and she worked for the Colton Plaza Hotel, he was her boss. He could even fire her.

"You don't trust me," he said.

"I don't know you," she said.

He uttered a sigh, as if that was a relief—that she didn't know him. But then he said, "Let's change that. Let's get to know each other." He entwined their fingers and tugged her along with him as he headed out of the ballroom.

"Where are we going?" she asked.

He stopped near the bank of elevators and pressed the up button. While he didn't live in the hotel, he had a suite reserved on the twenty-first floor. Was this why? Because he could pick up women as easily as he'd picked up her?

He turned back to her. "I want to see you under the stars," he said. "There's a bar on the roof, and a band. A better one than the conference has. I suspect that's where everyone has gone."

So he hadn't just assumed she'd go to his room. That was good. But she had to acknowledge a flash of disappointment. She wouldn't have been upset at being invited to see his suite. The night wasn't over yet. She'd just left the ball, and she didn't mind since she was leaving with the prince. The elevator doors swooshed open to a full car of rowdy-sounding guests. They must have been abandoning the quieter bar in the lobby for the rooftop lounge.

She stepped back, willing to wait for the next elevator. But Blake pulled her inside with him. As crowded as it was, they had to stand very close to each other—so close that they touched everywhere. Arm, hip, thigh…

A guest jostled Juliette, and her heel twisted, nearly twisting her ankle, as well, but Blake's arm slid around her waist, pulling her more tightly against him. Even after the doors opened and they exited onto the roof, Blake kept his arm around her.

He led her onto the dance floor and pulled her closer yet as he held her in his arms. They danced slowly— slower even than the beat of the music. It was as if Blake, too, wanted to savor every minute of the evening like Juliette did.

He stared at her so intently that she lifted a hand to her face and asked, "What's wrong?"

Had her makeup run down her face? She usually didn't wear this much, but her friend had applied it heavily, to make Juliette look older—like the accomplished businesswoman her fairy godmother had been.

Blake lifted her hand from her face and replaced it with his, sliding his thumb along her jaw. "You are so beautiful—" he uttered a wistful sigh "—more beautiful than the stars themselves…"

She smiled. Her prince was definitely charming. Not that he was hers…except maybe for this night. A night she intended to make the most of—while it lasted.

They danced until the band stopped for a break. Then Blake, his arm still around her, began to steer her toward the rooftop bar.

But Juliette saw who the bartender was, a young man she'd turned down for a date several times. If he recognized her and—given how he always stared at her—he probably would, she knew he would blow her cover and destroy her evening. So she dug in her heels and propelled them to a stop.

"Don't you want a drink after all that dancing?" Blake asked.

"Uh, yes…" Despite the cool autumn air blowing around the roof top, she was hot and flushed, but that was more from his closeness than from the dancing. "But not here…"

Blake glanced down at her. "Then where?"

She knew what he would think, but she didn't care. She didn't want her ball to end at midnight. She was greedier than Cinderella. She wanted longer than a few hours and more than a few dances. She wanted Blake. "Your room."

He stared into her eyes, and as he did, his pupils dilated, swallowing the green. Then, his arm around her, he led her back to the elevators. But a line had already formed for them. So he pushed open the door to the stairs. "It's just one flight down," he assured her.

But when her heel slipped on one of the steps, he swung her up in his arms. "We can't have you breaking an ankle," he murmured.

"I can take off the shoes," she offered. She didn't want to break an ankle, either, because when this evening was over, she would have to go back to her real life and her two jobs and mountain of bills.

"I have you," he assured her.

A wistful sigh slipped through her lips. She wished he had her, but he didn't even know her. If he did, he wouldn't be carrying her; he would be asking her for extra towels. But she wasn't going to worry about that now. She was just going to enjoy being treated like a princess. So she linked her arms around his neck and snuggled against him, brushing her lips over his throat.

His pulse leaped beneath her mouth, and he tensed. "Now *I* might slip," he murmured. But he was already on the landing, pushing open the door with his shoulder. A few strides down the hall and he stopped outside a door. "You'll need to take the key card from my pocket," he said, and his voice sounded strange, strangled.

She smiled and slid one hand over his ass.

He nearly jumped and cleared his throat. "Not that pocket. Inside jacket pocket."

So she moved her hand between them, pushing aside his jacket to run her fingers down his dress shirt and over the rippling muscles beneath the silk.

"You need to find that key," he said through gritted teeth, "quickly."

"Why?"

He showed her why—with his mouth. He lowered his head and brushed his lips across hers before deepening the kiss.

Passion coursed through Juliette, and she kissed him back with all the desire she felt for him. Her hands moved through his short, spiky dark gold hair as she held his head to hers.

His arms tightened around her, and he shuddered slightly. Lifting his mouth from hers, he panted for breath and murmured, "The key card…"

She fumbled inside his jacket until she found it. When she pulled it out, the card nearly slipped from her fingers. Blake caught it and swiped it through the lock. Then he pushed open the door and carried her over the threshold.

The significance of the gesture must have sobered him a little because he set her on her feet and closed the door. And as he did, he ran his hand through the hair she'd tousled. "I—I got carried away," he murmured, his face flushed.

"Uh, technically I was the one who got carried away," she said. "Or carried down…the stairs."

His sexy mouth curved into a grin. But the humor didn't entirely reach his green eyes; he still looked troubled. Maybe he'd changed his mind about bringing her to his room. He left her standing by the door as he headed to the bar on the other side of the large suite.

"Don't worry," she assured him. "I know you carrying me over the threshold doesn't make me your bride."

He shuddered at the thought.

She'd been so hot earlier—in his arms, with his mouth on hers. But now she was chilled.

"I'm sorry," he said. "It's just that I want nothing to do with marriage. My dad has had more than his share of marriages and I don't think any of them made him happy." His mouth pulled down into a frown now. "Actually I don't think anything makes him happy…except maybe his company and his money…"

"I'm sure that *you* do," she said. "That he loves you very much…" He had to be so proud of Blake; she'd heard that instead of going to work for Colton Energy with his oldest sister, Blake had launched his own successful start-up company straight out of business school.

He snorted. "You don't know my father," he said. "He doesn't love anyone but himself."

She'd heard that Fenwick Colton was one selfish son of a bitch. But how could he not love his own child?

She'd been feeling sorry for herself until now—until realizing that even though she'd lost her parents, at least she'd had no doubt that she had made them happy and that they had loved her.

His jaw was tense, a muscle ticking in his cheek. "I'm not going to make the mistakes he has. No marriage for me. No kids. Then nobody will feel like they don't matter as much as business does to me—because that is all that's going to ever matter to me."

He was warning her, but it wasn't a warning that she needed. She had no intention of getting married or having kids, either. She was taking criminal justice courses at community college because she wanted to be a cop, specifically a K9 cop. Her other job was helping out at the Red Ridge canine training center, and she loved working with the dogs.

"Maybe I'm more like my dad than I realized," he murmured. Along with Blake's words, she heard the pain and resentment in his voice. And she felt his pain, as well.

She stepped away from the door, crossing the room to where he stood by the bar with the wall of windows behind him, looking down on Red Ridge. Like she'd always thought he would look down on her.

But Blake Colton wasn't the spoiled, privileged prince she'd thought he would be. He was vulnerable and charming and incredibly handsome. He sighed and blew out a ragged breath. "I'm so sorry," he said. "I shouldn't be thinking about anything but how lucky I am."

She'd always thought he'd been born with a silver spoon in his mouth. But while he didn't have to worry about money, he had more emotional concerns.

He stepped closer and touched her chin. Sliding his fingertips along her jaw, he tipped her face up toward his. "I'm the luckiest man in Red Ridge that you came back to my room with me."

Her lips curved into a smile. And there was the charm again. Her prince…

She linked her arms around his neck again and pulled his head down for her kiss. She'd just felt his vulnerability, his pain, and she sought to soothe it with her lips and her passion. That kiss led to more—to making love the entire evening—over and over again.

But just before dawn, when Juliette had heard the creak and clatter of a cart in the corridor, she'd remembered who she was and that she had a shift to begin soon. So she'd slipped out of the arms of her sleeping prince, back into her dress and heels and into the hall.

Within minutes the dress and heels had been stowed in her locker, and she'd been back in her drab uniform of a Colton Plaza Hotel maid. Hours later, Blake had passed her in the hall while she was wearing that uniform, and he hadn't noticed her at all.

And she'd realized the night that had seemed so special to her was just a dream born of a silly fantasy. She was no Cinderella and Blake Colton was no prince charming. He would never try to find her and propose.

He'd made it all too clear what he thought of marriage and that he never intended to make the mistakes his father had made—with women or children.

So when she'd missed her period and taken that pregnancy test, she'd been reluctant to seek him out with the news that he was going to be the father he'd sworn he never wanted to become. She'd known he would be furious with her—maybe even think she'd tricked him.

But before she'd been able to build up her courage to confront him, she'd seen in the *Red Ridge Gazette* "People" section that he'd left Red Ridge and not just for a vacation. He intended to launch his start-up company in other countries and call it Blake Colton International.

International...

So why was he back in town?

He wanted to talk to Juliette. Why? What did he want from her? Their child? He'd vowed he'd never wanted to be a father. That was why, even when Elle had been urging her to tell him, Juliette had hesitated to seek him out. She hadn't wanted him to reject his child.

But he hadn't looked at Pandora like he was going to reject her. Juliette closed her eyes as fear overwhelmed her. Why had he wanted to see their daughter now—when she'd just witnessed a crime?

Now Juliette had to worry about losing Pandora to her father as well as to a killer.

# *Chapter 4*

Blake paced the suite on the twenty-first floor of the Colton Plaza Hotel. This was the same room where he'd spent that incredible evening with *Juliette*. He hadn't known her last name then. And after she'd slipped away from him, he hadn't even known if Juliette was her real first name or if she'd just been a Shakespeare fan. He'd had no idea who she really was. Hell, he still didn't know who she was or even if she would show up like he'd requested.

He stopped at the windows that looked down onto the lights of Red Ridge. He'd turned on only one of the lamps in the room, so his reflection stared back at him in the glass.

And he had to be honest. He hadn't requested that she come; he'd demanded. Maybe he was more like his old man than he'd thought—than he'd ever hoped to be. But then, he had every reason to make demands of Juliette. She'd been lying to him—that night all those years ago and every day since, when she'd kept his daughter from him.

The fury he'd felt when he'd seen her—with that child in her arms—coursed through him again. He was not going to spend another day in the dark. Hell, he was not going to spend another minute. He'd give her a little more time to show up tonight. Then he would track her down, and at least this time—unlike last—he knew where to look for her. At the Red Ridge Police Department...

She'd been wearing a uniform. She worked there. He shouldn't have left the building. He should have talked to his cousin Finn, but not about what was going on in Red Ridge. He should have asked him about Juliette and about what the hell crime her—*their*—daughter had witnessed.

How much danger were she and her mother in? Was that why Juliette hadn't shown up yet? Had something happened?

Too anxious for answers, Blake turned away from the windows and headed toward the door. When he jerked it open, he found her standing in the hall—as if she'd been trying to work up her nerve or her courage to face him.

He glanced around her, but she was alone. She hadn't brought the little girl or her dog. She wasn't wearing her uniform anymore, either. She'd changed into a khaki skirt and a loose blouse. It didn't matter what she wore—that glittery gown from years ago, the uniform or casual clothes—like a blonde doll getting dressed up in different outfits, she looked beautiful in anything.

But she was the most beautiful in nothing at all…

"You're here," he murmured, and instinctively he reached out to touch her, to see if she was real. Because when he'd thought about that night for the past five years, he'd always wondered if it had really happened or if it had just been some fantasy he'd conjured up.

Before he could brush his hand across her cheek, she flinched and stepped back. "That's not why I came here."

She must have thought he was making a pass. And he hadn't been—at least, not consciously.

"That's not why I asked you here," he said. He stepped back so she could enter the suite.

But she hesitated, as if she didn't believe him.

"Seriously," he said. "All I want from you is the truth. You damn well owe me that." She'd owed him that for the past five years.

She drew in a deep breath and stepped across the threshold, which reminded him of that night, of how he'd carried her across it and freaked out. She glanced up, met his gaze and nodded, as if she remembered it, too. "That's why," she said. "Even if I could have found you after you left town, I didn't think you'd want to know. You'd made it clear that you didn't want to be a father—ever."

He still didn't. But he didn't have a choice now. He was one. Wasn't he?

"So she is mine?"

She hesitated a moment, as if debating whether she could get away with lying about it.

"I'll ask for a paternity test," he warned her. No matter what she told him, he should do that anyway. But he didn't need one. That little girl looked like him—down to the dimple in her left cheek.

Color rushed to her pale skin as her face flushed. "She's yours."

He hadn't shut the door yet, so he looked into the hall again. Empty. "Why didn't you bring her?" he asked as he closed the door.

He hadn't chosen to be a father, but now that he was one, he wanted to know about his child. He wanted to see her, to talk to her, to hold her...especially when he remembered how upset she'd been at the police department. The tears, the fear...

Juliette's teeth sank into her bottom lip and she shook her head. And in her eyes were the same tears and fear that had been in her daughter's.

"What happened today?" he asked. "What crime did she witness?" He should have asked that earlier—should have demanded his answers then. But he'd been too stunned to think, to feel anything but shock.

"Murder," Juliette replied.

And that shock struck him again. He shook his head. "No..." He'd known there had been some murders in Red Ridge, but those had involved grooms. "Were you two at a wedding?"

Juliette shook her head. "We were at the park. She was sitting on top of the tall slide, and she saw a man and woman in the parking lot." She shivered. "She told me and the detective later what happened—that the woman opened a suitcase full of bags of sand and the man pulled out a gun and shot her. Then he threw the suitcase in the car and came after us." Her voice cracked with that fear.

And Blake instinctively reached for her again. But this time she didn't pull away. Instead she let him tug her into his arms and hold her as she trembled against him.

"What happened then?" he asked.

Obviously, she and the little girl had gotten away from the killer. But he wanted the details, needing to know how close he had come to losing them before he'd even known they were here.

"I hid Pandora in the tunnel under the slide…"

Pandora. That was the little girl's name.

"He didn't find her?"

"He found us," Juliette said. "But before he could shoot us, I shot him."

He shuddered now. He hadn't known her at all five years ago. She'd seemed so refined—so delicate—but she was much stronger than he'd known.

"I just grazed his shoulder, and he got away before I could arrest him," she said, her voice heavy with regret. "He told me that he'd get her, though. And I know that he will try. She saw him kill that woman."

That poor little girl. Nobody should have to witness something so horrific, let alone a child.

He pulled Juliette's trembling body even closer to his. But he wasn't sure whom he was trying to comfort now—her or himself. "Where is she?"

"The woman died."

"No," he said. "Your—our—" His voice cracked as he corrected himself, and he felt a rush of his own fear. "Our daughter," he continued. "Where is she?"

Juliette's breath shuddered out, brushing softly across his throat. Then she stepped back, out of his embrace, and wrapped her arms around herself. "I talked the chief into putting her in a safe house. The killer saw my uniform, so I'm sure he will be able to figure out who I am easily enough and where we live."

"You're in danger, too, then," he said, and he fought the urge to reach for her again, to hold her in his arms and keep her safe. "If he got close enough for you to shoot him, you saw him."

She nodded. "He was wearing sunglasses and a hood. But the hood blew back, and the glasses slipped down…" She shuddered again. "And I'll never forget that face, those eyes…"

He'd once said the same thing about her—that he would never forget her. And that had scared him, too, but no way near to the extent that she was afraid. She feared for her life. He'd feared only for his heart.

"So you can identify him," he said. Hopefully the Red Ridge Police Department could find the guy and put him behind bars for life for the life he'd taken.

"I looked through all the mug shots and—" she shook her head "—nothing. I thought he looked familiar, but I couldn't find any arrest or outstanding warrant for him." Her brow furrowed with frustration.

That same frustration coursed through him. Now there was more than one killer on the loose in Red

Ridge. But this killer wasn't after just grooms. He was after Juliette and Blake's daughter.

"I'm going to hire private guards to watch that safe house," he said. He'd heard of a reputable security firm out of River City, Michigan. He would hire the Payne Protection Agency to guard his little girl. He hadn't known he was a father until now—but now that he knew, he was going to do the best he could by his daughter.

Juliette shook her head. "That's not necessary. Red Ridge PD will protect her. She has an officer staying with her inside the house and another one patrolling outside it. She has police protection 24-7."

And what about Juliette? Who was protecting her? Nobody had been in the hall with her when she'd arrived. Was there anyone waiting outside to protect her? Or had she come alone?

Blake shook his head. "The department is spread too thin right now. Surely you must realize that—with a serial killer on the loose and then this…murder involving drugs…"

What the hell had happened to Red Ridge since he'd been gone? When he was growing up here, it used to feel like nothing ever happened—except for that one night. But now too much was happening in Red Ridge.

Too damn much crime…

Juliette's face flushed again, and finally she nodded in agreement. "Our resources are limited right now…"

And they were about to get more limited. That was another reason Patience had called him. If their father lost Colton Energy, Red Ridge would lose their funding for the K9 program, as well. His late first wife's trust had originally funded the program, and he'd taken over when that had run out.

If the program ended, then Juliette would probably lose her job—her way of supporting their daughter, which she'd been doing alone.

Until now.

"You'll have to run it past the chief, though," she cautioned him.

That wasn't all Blake intended to run past the chief. He intended to make sure Juliette had protection, as well. But he didn't bring it up now because he didn't want to argue with her while she was upset.

"He doesn't even want me going to visit Pandora at the safe house," she remarked, and there was a little catch in her voice, as if she was choking down a sob.

Blake reached for her again, pulling her against him. His body tensed as attraction overwhelmed him.

"I've never been separated from her before," Juliette said. "She's never spent a night away from me…"

And his attraction cooled as his anger returned. Now he stepped back, breaking the physical connection with her. And physical was all they would ever have—if that. She was a woman he would never be able to trust—not after how she'd misled him five years ago.

Obviously she had not been the rich businesswoman he'd thought she was. And then to keep his daughter from him…

"I can't say the same," he remarked resentfully. "All I've been is separated from her. You should have told me…"

"I told you why," she said, and she gestured at the

door and that threshold. "I didn't think you'd want to be part of her life."

He shook his head, rejecting her excuse. "I should have been given the chance to decide that for myself," he said. "You should have told me."

She shrugged. "You were already gone."

"But all my family is still in Red Ridge," he said. Except for his mother, who was always traveling. "You could have found me."

She snorted. "Like you tried to find me?"

"I told you, I tried," he said. "But after you snuck out in the middle night without even giving me your last name, I didn't have much to go on."

"You walked right past me," she said.

He laughed. Like that would have been possible. There was no way he wouldn't have noticed her, especially after that night. "When?"

"The very next day," she said. "Just out in the hallway." She gestured toward the door again. "But then, I didn't expect you to notice me. I was just the hired help."

He snorted now. "Yeah, right…in that dress, those heels…" The earrings. He still had those. She'd left them on the nightstand next to the bed.

"Those were a tip from a hotel guest," she said. "I was a maid here, putting myself through college."

He narrowed his eyes. "What was that night about?" Had she deliberately set out to seduce him? To get pregnant? But if that had been her plan, why hadn't she told him when she'd gotten pregnant?

If she'd been after money, that would have been the time for her to ask. But she'd never asked. She had raised their daughter all these years with no financial support from him. Unless she'd gotten it from someone else...

He narrowed his eyes and studied her face. "What were you after?"

Maybe it wasn't him at all. His father dated only younger women. Blake felt physically sick at the thought of her with Fenwick Colton.

"Nothing," she said. "I didn't want anything from you then and I don't want anything from you now."

"You already took something from me," he said. "My daughter—and nearly five years of her life."

Juliette flinched. "I'm sorry. I really didn't think you'd care..."

That night he'd told her so much—about his family— about himself. He'd been vulnerable with her in a way that he'd never been vulnerable with anyone else. Maybe she'd thought he was like his father despite his vow that he didn't want to be. Maybe she'd thought he was too selfish to care about his kids or anyone else.

"You should have let me decide," he said.

Her face flushed again, and she slowly nodded in agreement. "You're right. I'm sorry." Her voice cracked with emotion. "I can't give those years back to you, but I can show you pictures. Videos. Christmas and birthdays and Halloween parties."

His chest ached at the thought of all those milestones he'd missed. But photos and videos wouldn't tell him what he really wanted to know. "What is she like?"

Juliette's lips curved into a smile, and her already beautiful face became even more so as love radiated from within her. "She's amazing. So sweet. So generous. So funny…" She chuckled as if remembering something.

Something he'd missed. He'd missed a lot of somethings that nothing could bring back. No matter what she told him.

She shared stories with him. Story after story about something Pandora had done or said. And finally she must have noticed that while he listened, he said nothing. His heart ached too much over all the time he'd lost with his child.

She reached out now and ran her hand down his arm. "I'm sorry," she said again, and tears glistened in her blue eyes until she blinked them back. "I'm so sorry…" It was obvious she felt guilty now.

But Blake couldn't absolve her of that guilt. He couldn't change what had happened or get back those years he'd lost. And because of that, he would never be able to forgive her.

She had kept so much from him—his daughter and the truth about who and what she was. So he would never be able to trust her, either.

Finn looked pointedly at his wrist as he opened his condo door for his late-night visitor. He wasn't wearing a watch, though. He'd taken that off when he'd gone to bed a couple of hours ago. He was *not* happy that he'd had to leave his sexy, naked fiancée in that bed alone to answer the door.

Not that anyone knew he was engaged. Because of that damn Groom Killer, he and Darby were forced to keep their engagement secret. He suspected theirs wasn't the only secret engagement in town.

"What do you want, Blake?" He'd heard his billionaire cousin was back in Red Ridge, but he hadn't seen him yet. He could have waited until daylight for that. Maybe Blake was still on whatever time zone he lived in now.

"I need to talk to you about Juliette..."

"Walsh?" Finn finished for him. That was the only Juliette he knew.

Blake's handsome face twisted into a slight grimace as he nodded. "Yes, Walsh."

Finn wrinkled his brow. "How do you know that particular K9 cop?" Juliette's partner specialized in drug sniffing. Had Sasha gotten a hit on Blake?

A lot of spoiled rich kids got involved in drugs. But Blake, despite being the only male heir to the rich branch of the Colton family, wasn't spoiled. Finn knew he'd worked damn hard to establish his own business without his father's help. Maybe that was because he'd been trying to spite his father, though.

"I met Juliette before I left Red Ridge," Blake said—almost reluctantly.

"That was nearly five years ago," Finn remembered. "How would your paths have crossed? Juliette was working two jobs back then to pay off her mother's medical bills and put herself through college." He had a lot of respect for the young woman's work ethic. That was why he was damn happy to have her as part of his police force.

A ragged breath escaped Blake's lips. "I—I didn't know that..."

"So you didn't know her well, then," Finn said. Sounded like he hadn't even known her last name. "What's with your sudden interest in her now?"

"I—I know she and her daughter are in danger," Blake said. "And I want to help."

Finn furrowed his brow again. "That's not necessary." A civilian like Blake would only get in Finn's way. "I've got it handled. The little girl is in a safe house with around-the-clock protection—"

"Juliette should be in the safe house, too," Blake said. "With the child."

Finn nodded. "I tried that. She refused to go into hiding." He suspected she wanted to personally catch the killer who'd traumatized her daughter. "I'll have other officers watching her at all times."

Blake shook his head. "That's not enough. With all these murders, the Red Ridge PD is spread too thin."

Finn couldn't argue with that. He was damn tired of not being able to find Demi. He would have rather she was the cousin who had paid him this late-night visit, so he could figure out whether or not she was the Groom Killer. He suspected not, and there was a psycho on the loose in Red Ridge.

Then he also had the Larson twins and all the criminal activities he suspected they were behind to deal with, as well. He needed more than suspicions to nail them, though. He needed proof. But the officers he'd put on surveillance of the twins' real estate company hadn't come up with anything yet.

"We're spread a little thin," he reluctantly admitted. "But we protect our own. Nothing will happen to Juliette or her daughter." He would make damn sure of that.

Blake shook his head again, and there was a slightly wild look in his green eyes. Fear. He was really afraid for Juliette and Pandora. But why did a woman he'd barely known years ago matter so much to him?

"I'm hiring a private security company out of Michigan," he said. "I want to have bodyguards backing up the police at the safe house and the car following Juliette around."

Finn groaned. He didn't need outsiders getting in his way any more than he needed billionaire Coltons. He already had Blake's father breathing down his neck to find Demi; he didn't need Blake breathing down his neck, too. At least his father had a reason; he was worried about his business. Apparently his daughter was supposed to marry a zillionaire to save Colton Energy in a merger. But because of the Groom Killer, Layla Colton's fiancé had called off the necessary wedding.

What was Blake's reason?

So Finn asked, "Why do you care so damn much about a woman you must not have seen in five years?"

Blake's jaw clenched so tightly that a muscle twitched in his cheek—in his left cheek with the deep dimple in it. The same one Juliette's little girl had.

"She's yours," Finn said with sudden realization. "Juliette's daughter is yours."

Blake nodded.

"I didn't know…" Finn murmured. How had the Red Ridge rumor mill missed that juicy bit of gossip? Hell, how had the media?

"Neither did I," Blake replied.

And Finn flinched for him. Obviously, his cousin had just learned that he was a father—as his daughter was in danger. He reached out and squeezed his shoulder. "I don't know what to say, man…"

"Say that you'll accept my help," Blake said. "These bodyguards are the best."

Finn sighed.

"And along with the bodyguards, I intend to protect Juliette myself," Blake said.

Finn snorted.

Blake tensed, looking offended.

"Come on," Finn said. "You're no bodyguard." He was a billionaire.

"The bodyguards will be there, too," Blake pointed out. "So will your officers."

"Yeah, so you don't need to be," Finn said.

"Yes, I do."

And from the determination in his cousin's voice, Finn knew there would be no arguing him out of it. Even if he flat-out told him not to, he suspected Blake would follow her around anyway.

"Why?" he asked again. Blake's revelation explained why he wanted the extra protection on Pandora but not on Juliette. "Why would you put your life in danger for someone who didn't even tell you that you had a kid?"

Blake sighed. "This isn't about me. It's about that little girl. She can't lose the only parent she knows."

Finn echoed Blake's sigh in agreement. But he had to point out, "She might lose both of you since you're putting your life in danger, too."

# Chapter 5

"Why can't you come tuck me in, Mommy?" The question emanated from the speakers in Juliette's personal vehicle since her cell had connected via Bluetooth.

She wanted more than anything to be with her daughter, to hold her in her arms. She had only missed that first night of tucking Pandora into bed, but Elle had assured Juliette that the little girl had been so exhausted she'd fallen immediately to sleep. That was not the case tonight. Tonight, she was so upset that Elle had had to call Juliette to settle her down.

Pandora seemed to be getting more and more upset. She wanted to be with Juliette as badly as Juliette wanted to be with her. They were all each other had ever had. And it was killing Juliette to be away from her.

Last night Juliette had had a distraction—that meeting with Blake. It had gone better than she'd expected it would. While he had been angry with her, he hadn't been as furious as he could have been with her, as he probably should have been with her.

But he'd been too concerned about the danger she and Pandora were in to focus too much on what she'd done. On how she'd betrayed him. She had no doubt that, despite her apologies, he hadn't forgiven her, though.

He had just made keeping Pandora safe his top priority. But what would happen once the killer was caught? What would Blake do then?

He would want to meet his daughter. He deserved to meet his daughter. Yet right now that would be putting her at risk—just like Juliette visiting her would. That was why the chief had insisted that if she was determined to keep working, she couldn't go to the safe house. They couldn't risk the killer following Juliette to her daughter.

But when that soft voice emanated from the car speakers, breaking with sobs as she pleaded, "Mommy, come tuck me in..." Juliette worried that she'd made the wrong choice. Her heart ached with missing her little girl.

She'd thought that if she stayed on the job, she would be able to find the killer faster than her coworkers. After all, she'd seen him; they hadn't. Hell, she'd even hoped to draw him out, so that this would all be over soon. So that she and Pandora could go back to their everyday, perfect life together.

But even after the killer was caught, they wouldn't

be able to do that—because of Blake Colton. No matter what, he would be part of their daughter's life now. And that would make him part of Juliette's. He wouldn't be just a nearly five-year-old memory. Juliette focused on her daughter again. "Sweetheart, I wish I could be with you right now…"

But she loved her too much to put her in any more danger than she already was.

"I'm working right now, though, baby…"

A little hiccupping sob echoed throughout the car. "Did you get the bad man, Mommy?"

"Not yet, honey," she said. "But I will find him pretty soon. Then we can go home."

"I wanna go home now, Mommy!" Pandora said, and now her sobs became wails of frustration and anxiety.

Juliette's already aching heart threatened to break. She hated when her daughter cried, which, until the day before in the park, had been very rarely.

"Shh, shh," she tried to soothe the child. "Don't cry, sweetheart. We will be together again soon." They had to be. It was hurting Juliette as much as it was Pandora for them to be apart.

However, she didn't know if putting the killer behind bars would guarantee that they would never be separated again. What if Blake wanted visitation? What if he would be the one putting their daughter to bed on some nights? But his life wasn't here in Red Ridge; it was overseas, in various other countries, according to the tabloids. The same tabloids that had published photos of him with models and actresses and foreign royalty.

If not for Pandora, Juliette wouldn't have believed

that night had happened, because guys like Blake never noticed women like her. She wasn't famous or rich or well connected.

"You gotta catch the bad man, Mommy," the little girl pleaded. "You have to make sure that he doesn't make us dead like he said…"

"You are safe," Juliette promised her. "Nothing will happen to you."

"Are you safe, Mommy?"

Juliette had thought she was. She'd had a very uneventful day despite spending it on the streets, talking to informants, trying to find out if anyone knew anything about the man Pandora had witnessed committing a murder or at least about the purple-haired woman he'd killed. Since Pandora had seen her with a suitcase of drugs, she must have been a dealer. But nobody had been talking.

Yet. She would keep at them until they did.

But while she'd felt safe during the day, she had an odd sensation now. And Sasha, sitting in her harness in the back seat, must have felt it, too, because the beagle suddenly sat up and strained against the pet safety belt.

"Yes, of course I'm safe," Juliette assured her daughter. But then she noticed the glimmer of lights in the rearview mirror. She'd been driving for a while as she'd internally debated whether or not she should go to Pandora. So the routes she'd taken had been circuitous, leading toward neither her house nor the safe house. She'd just turned onto random roads until she found herself on the outskirts of Red Ridge in an area of greenhouses for one of the bigger plant nurseries. In July the greenhouses would be empty—too hot to use for the summer. So why were there lights behind her?

Who would be heading out this way? She didn't think the road led to any housing developments.

A knot of apprehension tightened in her stomach as she faced the likelihood that the vehicle was out there only because it had followed her.

Who? Was it the shooter? Or one of those people Juliette had questioned today? Maybe one of them was ready to talk to her.

She hoped that was the case, but she had to be prepared that it was the former. The killer carrying out the threat he'd made on the playground.

Her pulse quickened. While she was afraid, she was also—oddly—hopeful. Maybe she wouldn't have to search any longer to find him. Maybe he had found her.

The challenge was going to be taking him out before he could take out her. She couldn't leave her daughter alone. But then, Pandora wouldn't be alone. She had a father—a man she had never officially met, though.

"I have to go for now, honey," Juliette told her daughter as she flipped off the headlights and made a sharp turn around one of the empty greenhouses. "But I will see you soon."

As the vehicle following her also made the turn, she swallowed the fear that had rushed up on her. She hoped she would be able to keep that promise to her daughter. She hoped she would be able to see her again.

"Where the hell did she go?" Blake asked himself. She'd suddenly shut off her lights. But despite that, with the moon shining brightly, he'd been able to see her vehicle turn into the plant nursery. He'd followed it between two greenhouses. But her car was gone.

At least, he couldn't see it.

She couldn't have gone far. His lights shone onto the fields behind the greenhouse. The trees in it were seedlings—not big enough to hide a vehicle, even one as small as her economy sedan.

He drove a little farther—to the end of the greenhouse. Then he rolled down his window to peer around the back of the long building. He felt a sudden presence. From the corner of his eye, he caught the glint of moonlight shining off the barrel of a gun—the one pointed right at his head.

Maybe his cousin Finn had been right. Maybe he should have left the security detail to the professionals. But he hadn't even seen them following Juliette. He'd worried that she'd been left all alone.

"What the hell are you doing?" a female voice asked.

And now he kind of wished he'd left her alone. Juliette sounded furious with him. She pulled her gun back, sliding it into the holster on the belt of her uniform. She hadn't changed even though her shift had ended a couple of hours ago. But with the threat against her and her daughter, she would always be on duty.

Until the killer was caught.

"I'm following you," he said. He'd followed her all day as she'd gone from drug house to drug house. He knew she'd been looking for the killer or for information that would lead to him.

He was stunned that Red Ridge had areas like the

ones where she'd gone. Had things changed that much in the past five years? Or had he been so sheltered and self-involved all those years ago that he hadn't known those areas existed?

She uttered a sigh of pure exasperation. "I know you're following me. But why?"

"To protect you." His face heated now with embarrassment that he'd thought he could keep her safe. She was the one with a gun. His only weapon was his cell phone to call for help. For backup from the bodyguards and the police who were supposed to be following her. Where had they all gone?

She snorted. "How? By distracting me so I'll miss seeing the killer if he finds me?"

How was Blake a distraction to her? Was it just his presence? Or was it because of their past? Because of what they'd shared that night and what they had, unbeknownst to him, created? A child...

"I didn't mean to distract you," he said.

"Well, you did..." Then she muttered something else, something that suspiciously sounded like, "You've been doing it for years..."

But he hadn't been around for years. Had she thought of him as often as he'd thought of her? Probably not—because he'd thought about her all the time.

He pushed open the driver's door to step out of his car. But she caught and held it.

"Get back inside," she told. "Turn this car around and leave me alone."

He sucked in a breath, not at her rejecting him—or at least not entirely because of that—but because of the thought of her being alone. Physically he was stronger than she was, so he managed to open the door. But he was careful that he didn't hit her with it; he did propel her back a bit, though. Then he stepped out and shut the door—so there was nothing between them but a few feet of night air. He wanted to wrap his arms around her to protect her, but he was also furious with her.

"What the hell are you doing?" he asked her. "Why are you out here alone?"

Where were the bodyguards and the patrol car? he wondered again. They were supposed to be following her, too, and because of that, they were all aware of the make, model and license plate number of his rental vehicle.

He glanced around and noticed a faint glow of lights on the other side of one of the green houses. The tightness in his chest eased a little. They were here. She had backup.

She hadn't answered him. Had she noticed the glow of lights, too? Maybe those were from her car, though. He still couldn't see where she'd parked it. But it must have been close because he heard the low growl of her dog.

She must have, too, because she cocked her head and listened. And in the moonlight her brow furrowed.

"You aren't meeting someone out here, are you?" he persisted. "I thought your shift ended hours ago."

"It did," she said. "But I didn't want to go home..."

To an empty house. He could hear the pain in her voice, the ache of missing her daughter.

He felt both a twinge of sympathy and one of resentment. She knew their daughter enough to miss her. He didn't even know the child.

"And Elle called me for Pandora," she continued. "She wants to see me."

"Finn thinks it's too dangerous," Blake said, "that someone could follow you."

She sighed. "I guess he's right. You followed me."

"But you noticed me," he pointed out.

Her lips curved into a slight smile as the moonlight bathed her face with a golden glow. "You're not a professional," she said. "You shouldn't be trying to protect me. You're only going to get hurt."

"Too late," he murmured. He already was—hurt over all the years he'd missed with his daughter.

The smile slipped away, and she closed her eyes. "I'm sorry…"

She knew what he was talking about—what he would probably never get over—because no matter what, he couldn't get back those years he'd lost. He just had to make sure he didn't lose any more with her.

"Do you think Finn would let me see her?" Blake asked.

Juliette gasped. "The chief knows? You told him?"

That twinge of resentment spread to an ache. "I'm not keeping a secret that never should have been one in the first place."

Juliette's teeth sank into her bottom lip as if she was physically holding back a protest.

"What are you worried about?" he asked. "What people will think of you?"

She shook her head. "I don't care what people think. I didn't grow up like you. I grew up in the poor area of

Red Ridge. People always thought I was trash. So they can't think any worse of me than that."

Trash? He could not reconcile that impression with the one he'd carried of her the past nearly five years—of her in that glittery gown with those high heels and dangling earrings. She'd looked like a movie star. Or a princess…

Cinderella. That was who she'd been. His Cinderella…

But he hadn't been able to find her. Until now…

"I'm worried about Pandora," she said. "I don't want her in any more danger than she already is."

"So you want to keep me away from my daughter even longer?" he asked.

"I want to keep the killer away from her," Juliette said. "If he learns that you're her father—and once word gets out it will be all over the news—then he could follow you to her if you try to see her."

And he couldn't deny that he could probably be easily followed. But Juliette wasn't the only one missing their daughter. She was missing her after just one day. He was missing five years.

But could he take the risk that he might put her in more danger than she already was? No.

This was a hell of a risk. But he had to take it; he had no choice. The longer the K9 cop and her little kid lived, the greater the chance they would identify him. He needed to get rid of her now.

She wasn't alone, though.

He wasn't the only one who'd followed her to the plant nursery. She'd led a damn parade here. So he had to be very careful when he took the shot. He had to make sure it counted—that it killed her—and that he had time to get away before anyone saw him.

Like those other guys, he'd been following her the whole damn day from the time she'd left the Red Ridge Police Department that morning. She'd spent the day shaking things up—talking to informants, visiting drug houses.

He knew why.

She was trying to find him, or at least someone who would tell her who he was. Hopefully all those people were too scared, not just of him but of the people who'd hired him, to talk. But they were drug users, and so they were unpredictable.

He couldn't risk that someone might talk to her. He had to get rid of her. *Now.*

He stared through the scope of the long gun, trying to center her in the middle of it. But that damn guy kept getting in the way…

Who the hell was he? And why was he following her?

Beyond some mild curiosity, it didn't really matter to him who the guy was, though. If he got in the way of the shot, he was going to be dead—like the beautiful K9 cop. And soon her cute little kid would be dead, too.

He put his finger on the trigger.

# Chapter 6

The rumble of Sasha's low growl rose to a howl. And Juliette reached for the weapon she'd holstered—apparently too soon.

"Somebody already followed you here," she said as she gazed around the shadows the greenhouses cast.

She'd seen a faint glow a while ago—other lights shining on the premises. It could have been a motion light clicking on, or a vehicle's low beams from the other side of one of the greenhouses.

If someone had followed him here, there was no way she would let Blake anywhere close to Pandora's safe house—she didn't give a damn what her boss said about it. The little girl was not the chief's kid. But she was his cousin...

Juliette sucked in a breath with that sudden realization. And now her boss knew—thanks to Blake going to him behind her back.

"They didn't follow me," he replied. "Finn has a patrol car on you."

Members of her own team…

Juliette expelled the breath she'd sucked in—feeling like she'd been punched.

"And I hired that private security company like I told you I would," he said.

But she hadn't thought the chief would actually agree to Blake bringing in outsiders. And how had they gotten to Red Ridge so quickly?

"There are extra guards on both Pandora and you," Blake said.

She flinched. Did nobody think she could take care of herself? Not even her own coworkers, who should know her best? Sure, all the male ones were big and muscular, and she was not. But they shouldn't underestimate or think she was weak just because she was short and small-boned.

"You can come out!" she called to them. "I know you're all there…"

Nobody rushed out of the shadows, though, as if they weren't sure they were supposed to show themselves. What kind of orders had the chief given her fellow officers? And what had Blake told the bodyguards?

She could understand his hiring extra protection for their daughter. But why had he hired guards for her? And why the hell was he following her around himself?

He wasn't a cop or even a bodyguard. He was going to get himself killed.

And just as she thought it, she glimpsed the flash of a gun blast in the dark. The bullet struck the metal of his rental car just as she knocked Blake to the ground. Another bullet struck the mirror, raining shards of glass down on them. More bullets followed, striking the side of the car right above where they crouched.

He rolled so that she was under him, so that he was protecting her. But she was the cop.

"Let me up," she said.

Despite the situation, despite her frustration, she noted the heat and hardness of his muscular body. Maybe he was more capable of protecting her than she'd realized. He wasn't some soft billionaire. He was strong.

But so was she…

She shoved him off and turned her gun toward the direction from which the shots had come. She knew none of her fellow officers had fired those shots. Nor would bodyguards who'd been hired to protect her.

The shots had to have come from the killer. Along with everyone else, he must have been following her. She fired into the darkness and heard glass breaking as she struck a greenhouse. He must have gotten inside one of them. Or maybe he'd been on top of it.

She needed to check. But when she tried to get to her feet, Blake grabbed her and held her down. "You can't go after him," he said.

"It's my job," she reminded him.

"You're not going after him alone," another voice chimed in as K9 cop Dean Landon rushed up around the rear bumper of Blake's now bullet-ridden rental. He was the explosives expert, but since they didn't often have to deal with bombs in Red Ridge, it wasn't a surprise that the chief had tapped him for this secret assignment.

Tailing Juliette…

Like her, he must have left his dog in his vehicle. She would have released Sasha from her harness and taken her from the car if she thought the beagle could help locate the shooter. But she wasn't sure Sasha had been close enough to him in the park to recognize his scent.

Dante Mancuso joined them near the rear bumper. Unfortunately, he hadn't brought his dog, either. Flash, the bloodhound, was their evidence recovery dog. He'd been brought to the murder scene at the park. "I nearly just took out a couple private security guards," Dante said. "What the hell is going on here?"

"He hired them," Juliette said, gesturing at Blake.

"Well, they're going after the shooter," Dante said.

Juliette shook her head. "No, he's mine."

He'd threatened her and her daughter. She wanted to be the one to put the cuffs on him. She couldn't take the time for Dante to get Flash or even for her to get Sasha. She had to find the killer before the bodyguards did.

"You stay with Colton here," she told Dante. "Make sure he keeps his head down and doesn't get it blown off…"

"Juliette!" Blake protested. "You can't go out there! You're the one he's trying to kill."

"Exactly," she said.

When Blake reached for her again, Dante stepped forward and pushed him back onto the ground. She trusted that her coworker would protect the civilian. And as she headed out, crouching low and keeping to the shadows, Dean Landon crept along beside her. Like a bodyguard, he kept his body between hers and that greenhouse.

The shooting had stopped. The bodyguards must not have found him yet. Or he'd gotten away just like he had in the park even after she'd put a bullet in his shoulder.

Damn it...

Juliette couldn't have come this close to capturing him and he had already slipped away because of Blake because he'd held her back. If Blake truly wanted to help her and their daughter, the best thing he could have done was stay the hell out of her way.

"You can't let her go!" Blake yelled in protest as he strained against the hands holding him back. But this cop was a big guy. And he was armed.

"No," the police officer replied. "I can't let *you* go."

Frustration and fear gripped Blake in equal force, threatening to tear apart his madly pounding heart. He'd never been shot at before. And the bullets had come close, breaking the side mirror that had been just above his head and piercing the metal of the rental vehicle.

Juliette had saved his life. But now she was putting her own in danger.

"She can't go out there!" Blake protested. "He's going to kill her!" Those bullets had been meant for her—not him.

"Walsh is a good cop," the guy replied in her defense. "She knows what she's doing. Unlike you..."

Blake flinched. He had never been more aware—when those shots had rung out—that he was out of his element. His element was business, making deals and making money. Not getting shot at…

"The chief warned us that you were probably going to get killed," the guy continued.

Since the police officers backing her up had known about him, why hadn't she? Before Blake could ask him why the chief would have kept such a secret from her, shots rang out again.

Blake jumped up, his every instinct compelling him to run in the direction Juliette had gone and make sure she was all right. But he'd made it only a few feet when the cop knocked him to the ground. And when he tried to get up, a knee settled into his back.

"Stay the hell down," the guy told him. "Or I will damn well cuff you to this car."

That could have been just as dangerous as Blake going after Juliette. But the shots weren't coming anywhere near him now. They were on the other side of the greenhouse—maybe even on the other side of the one next to that one—because they weren't as close or as loud as they'd been when those bullets had nearly struck him.

He closed his eyes and hoped like hell those bullets weren't striking anyone now. Unless that anyone was the killer who'd threatened Juliette and their daughter. Blake didn't care what happened to that man as long as he was stopped.

But he was worried about Juliette and the others.

"Go," he urged the police officer. "Go help them. I'll stay here."

The officer rolled him over and studied his face through narrowed eyes. "I don't think I should trust you."

"I won't get in the way," Blake promised. Not any more than he already had. If Juliette hadn't noticed him following her, she never would have led him to this area—which had presented the killer with the perfect place to go after her.

More shots rang out. And the officer must have been more concerned about his coworkers than he was Blake, because he eased off him. Withdrawing his weapon from the holster on his belt, he headed toward the direction of all that gunfire.

Before Blake had left Red Ridge, he'd held a concealed weapons permit. He'd only applied for it so he would have something in common with his father. He'd thought that once he'd gotten it, his father might take him shooting like he did his business associates. But Fenwick had never invited him along to the range. No matter what Blake had done to get his attention, his father had never given it to him. When Blake had left Red Ridge, he had left the gun and the permit in the safe at his father's house.

He needed them now. He needed to be armed so he could protect Juliette. He only hoped that it wasn't already too late.

For the second night in a row, Finn's sleep was interrupted. But it was his phone ringing, not his doorbell. He fumbled around the bedside table until he grabbed up his cell and accepted the call.

"Chief Colton," he murmured groggily as Darby murmured in her sleep next to him. He slipped out of bed and walked into the hall so he wouldn't wake her.

She worked so damn hard that she needed her rest.

What the hell time was it?

Who would be calling him now?

If it was Blake or, worse yet, Fenwick…

But the voice on the other end was the gruff one of Frank Lanelli, the Red Ridge dispatcher. "Chief, we've got an officer down…"

And Finn's heart lurched in his chest. This was the call he'd never wanted to receive.

"How bad?" he asked, and his voice cracked slightly as concern overwhelmed him.

Lanelli's voice was gruff, too. "I don't know. It didn't sound good when the call came in. I dispatched the closest ambulance to the scene."

What scene? What the hell had happened? He wanted all the details, but most important, he wanted to know if his officer would survive.

"Do you have ETA?" Finn asked. Fortunately he'd left his clothes in the living room from when Darby had undressed him earlier. So he was able to pull them on without disturbing her.

"Hopefully they're en route to the hospital now."

And not the morgue…

He wanted to ask who the officer was, but he was afraid that he might already know.

Juliette…

She shouldn't have insisted on staying on the job.

She should have gone into the safe house with her daughter. Now she might not ever get the chance to see her little girl again.

## Chapter 7

The minute the waiting room doors opened—everyone jumped up from their seats and rushed toward the chief, who had just arrived at the hospital. But Juliette was already on her feet since she'd been pacing back and forth across the tile floor. So she beat everyone else to Finn Colton.

His blue eyes widened in surprise at seeing her. "It's not you…" he murmured. "The officer down…"

"Dean Landon," she replied. But it should have been her. That was who the killer had been aiming for, but Dean had been in the way. Just like Blake had been when the first shots had rang out.

"How is he?" Finn asked anxiously, his face tight with concern.

Juliette shrugged, her shoulders aching with the

weight of her guilt on them. "We don't know yet. He's still in surgery."

"What about Mancuso?" the chief asked as he glanced around the waiting room. "Is he okay?"

"He stayed behind with Flash to process the scene and collect whatever evidence the shooter might have left behind." She doubted he'd left any. He hadn't at the park. They had nothing but her and Pandora's description of him in order to identify him.

Because of the other officers gathered around, she lowered her voice and said, "You shouldn't have put a patrol on me." She glanced toward where Blake stood apart from everyone else, leaning against one of the brick exterior walls of the waiting room. "And you shouldn't have let him follow me around, either…"

"There was no stopping him," Finn replied. "Just like there was no stopping you. You need to be in that safe house with your daughter."

"I would have been fine," she insisted. "If I'd known I was being followed, I wouldn't have stopped."

Finn flinched, but he didn't acknowledge that she was right—even though they both obviously knew she was.

"You didn't know you were being followed," he said.

She flinched as she realized what she'd admitted. But she had been distracted—thanks to Blake—not inept.

Her boss must have thought she was the latter, though, because he added, "That's why you need backup."

She glanced again at Blake. Despite the dark circles of exhaustion beneath his eyes, he was still so damn handsome that her heart skipped a beat with the attraction that had never died—despite all the years. "I don't need *him* getting in my way. Why would you allow a civilian…"

Finn held up a hand to stop her protest. And he reminded her, "I'm the chief."

He was also Blake's cousin. Was he angry with her, like Blake was, for keeping Pandora a secret?

"I'm sorry," she said. And she was—sorry about so many things. At the moment, she was sorriest about Dean getting hurt. "It's my fault…"

"It's the shooter's fault," Finn said. "We need to find him."

"That's why I want to stay on the job," she said. "Why I don't want to stay at the safe house."

"You need to," a deep voice said, close to her ear.

The man's warm breath made her shiver. Then she tensed as she realized Blake had crossed the room without her noticing. He stood beside her now, so close that she could feel the tension in his body. The same tension that was in hers.

She shook her head. "And lead the killer right to…" *my daughter*… She couldn't say that at the risk that he might correct her and say she was *their* daughter—right in front of most of the Red Ridge Police Department. "… Pandora."

His handsome face was tense, as if it was killing him not to claim the child. But he had to be aware that everyone was watching them, already wondering what the hell he was doing there and what he was to Juliette.

"The bodyguards—they can make sure you get to her safely—with no one following you," he assured her.

She knew they were good. Right before the shots had started, Dean had been telling her that while he and Dante had easily made Blake's tail, they hadn't noticed the bodyguards until the guys had started to approach them at the plant nursery.

"She called you," Blake reminded her. "She wants to see you."

And her heart ached to see her little girl—especially after what had happened tonight. If Dean hadn't taken that bullet, she might not have had the chance to be with her daughter again.

"Those guards are good," the chief agreed. "They can take you to see her—if you want…" But he wasn't talking just to Juliette now. He was looking at Blake, as well.

She felt a twinge of panic that Finn knew. Who else had he told? Anyone? Everyone?

She felt like a fool over that night—over ever thinking that billionaire Blake Colton could be her Prince Charming. Or that she was Cinderella.

She was no princess. She was a cop. "I'm not going to stay there," she warned them both. "I have to find this killer…" Now more than ever, after one of her friends had been hurt because of him—because of her. "And I have to make sure Dean will be okay…"

Like everyone else, she was so worried about the fallen officer. Maybe that was why nobody asked her about Blake and what was going on between them. Or maybe some of them had already put it together—how long Blake had been gone and how old Pandora was…

It was inevitable that the little girl's paternity was

eventually revealed. Juliette had already had to tell the child that her daddy wasn't dead—just that he lived very far away.

He wasn't far away anymore, though.

In fact, he was much too close. So close that he could have been in surgery just like Dean Landon. If she hadn't seen that muzzle flash in the dark…

If she hadn't knocked him to the ground…

She shivered, and he slid his arm around her, as if to warm or comfort her. But conscious of everyone watching them, Juliette pulled away. While she didn't want him dead, she was furious with him for putting himself in that position—for putting himself in danger.

The officer's surgery had taken a long time—so long that the sun was already coming up as Blake and Juliette left the hospital. Not that they could see much more than a glimpse of it since they'd been zipped into black bags. They were rolled on stretchers out of the morgue and lifted into the cargo area of a long van. The minute the double doors closed, Blake jerked down the tab of the zipper and freed himself. Usually small spaces didn't bother him, but being zipped alive into a body bag was something from his worst nightmares.

He shuddered as he pushed it down around his shoulders and sat up. Juliette had unzipped hers, as well, and she sat across from him with her back against one of the metal sides of the van. There were no windows in the back and a solid partition between the front seat and the cargo area, so nobody could see them. He kicked off the bag and shuddered again.

"You could have wound up in one of these for real," Juliette warned him, her blue eyes suspiciously bright, as if she was about to cry.

But he doubted she cared enough to cry over him. She was probably upset about her friend.

"Officer Landon is going to be okay," he reminded her.

She sighed. "Not for a while."

The doctor had warned all his coworkers that he had a long recovery ahead of him. While Finn and Juliette had griped about the security agency Blake had hired, he was even happier that he had since the Red Ridge PD was going to be stretched even thinner than it had already been. He was also glad that the security firm could help reunite mother and child.

While he was determined to stick close and protect Juliette, he wasn't convinced that his meeting the little girl was a good idea. His stomach knotted with nerves. He trusted that the security firm would make sure the killer didn't follow them. He was nervous about meeting the child—his child. He had no experience with kids. He didn't know what to say to her, how to act.

Hell, he didn't know what to say to her mother or how to act, and Juliette was an adult. She was stubborn but also strong and brave. She'd been that way all those years ago—confident beyond her years.

Was that because of her mother's illness? He wanted to ask her about it—about all the medical bills Finn had said she'd been working two jobs to pay. Why hadn't she asked him for money back then? She could have, and he would have given it to her. Hell, after that night, he would have given her anything.

But his heart…

After watching his father's failed attempts at marriage and love, Blake knew they weren't for him. He'd also decided never to be a father, but now he was. He didn't have to get involved, though.

He didn't have to be part of her life. She and Juliette had done just fine without him all these years. But now that he knew…he couldn't just walk away. He couldn't pretend that he didn't have a child—like his father had pretty much done Blake's entire life. Sure, he'd acknowledged him and his sisters from time to time, but never with any real attention.

Even if he was bad at this, he still had to be better than his father was. But would he be good enough for a little girl who'd already been traumatized?

Juliette stared at him, as if she was watching all those doubts and fears cross his face. "Do you want to do this?" she asked him.

Those doubts and fears rushed up, choking him, so that he could only nod in response.

"What do you want to tell her?" she asked.

"The truth," he replied as he internally battled back his doubts and fears. "It's been kept for far too long."

She flinched but then persisted, "And what is the truth, Blake? Do you want to be part of her life? Do you want to be a father?"

"I am a father," he said. He wasn't certain how to be one, but he would have to figure it out.

"I'm not sure this is the best time to tell her that," Juliette said. "Not after what she's been through, the danger she knows she's—"

"Maybe having a father will make her feel safer." Having a father hadn't meant a whole hell of a lot to him. But then, he hadn't meant a whole hell of a lot to his father, either.

"She knows she has one," Juliette said.

At least she hadn't told the child he was dead.

"She just doesn't know who he is," Juliette continued.

"Then I would say that it's time she found out who I am, and that I will be here for her," Blake said.

Juliette narrowed her eyes. "For how long? Are you staying in Red Ridge?"

He flinched now. He hadn't even wanted to come back for a visit, but Patience had convinced him. "I can be her father whether I'm here or abroad."

Her lips drew into a tight line of disapproval. And he knew what she was thinking—the same thing he was—that he was going to be about as involved in Pandora's life as his father had been in his.

He flinched now. Maybe the best thing he could do for the little girl was continue the lie. But he knew how he felt over the truth being kept from him all these years—how betrayed he felt. He couldn't do that to the child.

The van stopped, idling, as something rattled open. Then the van lurched forward before stopping again. The ignition shut off. And something rattled closed. Moments later those back doors opened, but there was still very little light. They were in a garage, parked next to another vehicle. It must have belonged to the officers guarding Pandora.

"We're here?" he asked.

The bodyguard—a burly former Marine—nodded. "Yes, Mr. Colton." The guy reached up to help Juliette down from the back, but she ignored his hand and leaped down on her own.

She was so independent. Too independent.

Why had she never told him about their daughter? She'd already been struggling with her mother's bills. Why hadn't she at least sought him out for financial support?

He ignored the proffered hand and jumped down, as well. "Is it too early?" he asked her. "Will we be waking her up?"

Juliette smiled, transforming her already beautiful face to breathtaking. "She's an early riser. Even on my days off, she doesn't let me sleep in."

The door between the house and the garage opened, and a young woman breathed a sigh of relief before reholstering her weapon. "I'd hoped that was you!"

The two women embraced.

Blake recognized her as the Red Ridge officer who'd helped Juliette with Pandora at the police department. They seemed like more than coworkers, though. It was clear they were very close friends, especially when the woman glanced at him, and said, "You told him."

Juliette nodded.

And Blake stepped forward with his hand outstretched. "Yes, she told me," he said. "I'm Blake Colton." He was certain that she already knew, though.

There was an ironic twist to the curve of her lips when she replied, "Yes, I know. I'm Elle Gage." She took his hand and squeezed it. Like Juliette, she was stronger than she looked, and she was obviously trying to send him a message.

Probably not to hurt her friend.

He couldn't hurt someone who didn't care about him. If Juliette had cared, she wouldn't have kept his daughter from him for all these years. But he doubted Elle had had anything to do with that.

She had enough troubles of her own.

He extended his condolences to Elle. "I'm sorry to hear about Bo." When Patience had called to compel him to come home, she'd told him about everything that had happened in Red Ridge—about Bo Gage, the first victim of the Groom Killer, getting murdered the night of his bachelor party. "Was he a very close relative of yours?"

"My brother," she said, and sadness darkened her brown eyes. "I'm surprised you heard about it with how far you live away from here."

"My sister Patience called and told me about it," he explained.

"Everybody thinks Demi Colton did it," she told him, and there was an almost accusatory note in her voice. "She and Bo had been a couple until he broke up with her for another woman."

Oh, God, the last thing Red Ridge needed was the old feud between the Coltons and the Gages firing back up. But that sounded exactly like what Bo's murder had started. Blake just shrugged.

He wasn't part of that. He didn't live in the past like most of this town did. But as a little girl peeked around

Elle, he felt a pull to the past—wishing he could go back and reclaim the years he'd lost with her.

"Mommy!" she cried out, and she slipped around the female cop to throw herself into her mother's arms.

Juliette picked her up and spun her around, holding her close. And the look on her face…

It took Blake's breath away. He had never seen such a look of love. It stunned him.

"Mommy! Mommy!" she said as she pulled back and put her tiny hands on either side of Juliette's face. "I missed you…"

The wealth of emotion in those three words pulled at Blake, making his chest ache. He could see how true it was as tears sparkled in the little girl's eyes.

Juliette leaned her forehead against her daughter's and said, "I missed you, too, sweetheart." Then she kissed the little girl's nose.

Pandora wrinkled her nose and giggled. "Can we go home now, Mommy?"

Juliette's lips lowered in a frown. "Not yet, baby…"

"You haven't caught the bad man yet?" the child asked, and now the tears in her green eyes were tears of fear.

Anger surged through Blake. He wanted to take down that killer himself. And now he understood Juliette's insistence in staying on the job—in trying to find the man who'd threatened their daughter.

"Not yet, honey, but we're getting closer…"

He wasn't so sure about that. The killer had gotten close to her last night—too close when he'd shot the man right next to her.

"I heard about Dean," Elle remarked. While she kept her voice calm for the little girl's sake, anger shone in her eyes.

If the killer was smart, he would get the hell out of Red Ridge now. He was an even more wanted man than he'd been from the shooting in the park. Now he'd shot an officer.

"Dean will be fine," Juliette assured her friend.

Blake glanced back at her and noticed Pandora was staring at him. Was this it? Was this when he needed to introduce himself? What the hell would he say?

But then she asked, "Are you my daddy?"

And everyone gasped in surprise.

"I heard Auntie Elle say you live far away." Apparently the little girl had been standing behind the officer longer than they'd realized. She continued, "And my daddy lives far away."

So Juliette hadn't lied to their daughter.

All three females stared at him, waiting for his reply. He swallowed hard, choking down the emotion rushing up on him. "Yes," he answered her. "I am your daddy."

A long silence followed his acknowledgment. Then Pandora extended her arms toward him, angling away from her mother. For a moment he didn't know what she wanted—until he realized she was reaching for him.

He lifted her from Juliette's arms.

He didn't know much about children, but he suspected Pandora was small for her age. She was so light. He barely felt the weight of her in his arms, but he felt it in his chest, weighing heavily on his heart.

As she had with her mother, she reached up and

planted each of her tiny hands on the sides of his face. And she studied him intently as if trying to figure out if they looked alike. And they did.

Or maybe she was trying to discern what kind of man he was. A bad man like the guy who'd killed the woman in the park. Or a good man.

Blake wasn't always sure what he was. He wasn't a killer. But he could be quite cutthroat in business. Some women might claim he was the same with personal relationships. But before and after that night, no one had ever affected him like Juliette had.

A little finger traced over the dimple in his cheek. "I have a dent in my face, too," Pandora said.

"It looks better on you," he said.

"You're handsome," she said. "Just like Mommy said…"

He glanced at Juliette, who flushed a bright red while Elle chuckled. Curious, he asked, "What did Mommy tell you about me?"

"She told me that my daddy was a handsome prince who swept her off her feet." Her mouth curved down into a frown of disapproval. "Why would you knock Mommy down?"

"I picked her up," he said. "I didn't knock her down."

Elle laughed harder and murmured, "That might be a little too much information…"

"He carried me," Juliette clarified. "Because I almost tripped on some stairs…"

Pandora wasn't paying attention to either of the women. She was totally focused on him.

So he felt compelled to say, "I would never hurt your mommy. Or you…"

"Mommy said you left Red Ridge before she could tell you about me."

He glanced at Juliette again, wanting to convey his appreciation that she hadn't lied to their daughter. She could have let Pandora believe that he'd wanted nothing to do with her, especially since that was what she'd thought after the things he'd said that night, that he never wanted to be a husband or a father.

But Juliette wouldn't look at him.

So he focused on their daughter again. "I would have come back sooner," he said, "if I'd known about you." And he gently tightened his arms around the little girl, holding her close to his heart.

She settled her head onto his shoulder and emitted a soft sigh. "I'm glad you're back now," she said. "You can protect me and Mommy from the bad man."

He would damn well try his hardest to guard them— even if his efforts had him ending up in one of those body bags again.

# Chapter 8

"By now you've all heard about Officer Dean Landon," the chief said as he began the morning meeting.

Juliette glanced around the squad conference room. Every Red Ridge PD officer had been at the hospital the night before—whether they'd just stopped to check on him during a shift or they had come in while off duty. They had definitely all heard about Landon getting shot.

Did they blame her for it? Nobody was looking at her, but it was almost as if they were making a conscious effort not to. Maybe they knew she already felt guilty enough over what had happened to their coworker.

"Officer Landon is expected to fully recover from the gunshot wound," the chief assured them. "However, it will take some time, so I will be actively looking for a temporary replacement for him during his recovery."

Juliette expelled a breath. That was good. They couldn't be shorthanded right now.

"Until I find that temporary replacement, I need you all to pull together like never before," the chief continued. "No more infighting."

Juliette felt no guilt over that; she wasn't part of the feuding going on within the department because she was neither a Gage nor a Colton. It seemed as if, with a few exceptions like Dean Landon and Dante Mancuso and her, everyone in the K9 unit of the RRPD was related to one or the other.

"Have you heard from your sister?" Detective Carson Gage asked Brayden Colton, who was sitting in the chair in front of Juliette in the briefing room.

Brayden didn't answer him. Everyone knew Carson was romantically involved with a Colton—Serena, who'd become close to Demi before she'd fled. Serena believed in her innocence. But Carson was ambivalent. Unlike the detective, though, Brayden was sure his sister was not the Groom Killer. He thought she'd been framed.

From what Juliette knew of Demi Colton, she had to agree with him. If Demi had killed someone, she would have done a better job of covering her tracks. Not that she hadn't had a motive to kill Bo Gage. Apparently, he'd gotten her pregnant and then become engaged to another woman.

"Have you heard from her?" the chief asked now. "Any texts? Calls?"

The last time Demi had texted one of her brothers, she'd insisted she was innocent—and had said the baby was fine. No one could she be sure if she'd actually given birth yet, though the timing was right. Brayden shook his head. "No. And it's been a while..."

Juliette could hear the concern in his voice. His sister was on the run—alone, heavily pregnant or traveling with an infant, and desperate. Juliette knew how that felt. Compassion compelled her to reach out and squeeze his arm.

"I'm worried something could have happened to her," he admitted. "To them..."

"And whose fault would that be?" Carson asked.

"Her baby is a Gage, too," Brayden reminded the detective. "Do you want to lose another one?"

Carson flinched.

"Knock it off," the chief said. "After what happened to Dean last night, we all have to trust that we have each other's backs. I can't send any of you out there until I know that for certain."

Carson closed his eyes and nodded. "I'm sorry. Of course, I know that. And I do..." He looked across the aisle of chairs at Brayden. "I have your back."

"Juliette's the one we need to watch right now," the chief directed.

"You should be in witness protection with your daughter," Carson told her. "Not out trying to do my job to track down that killer."

"I will be able to recognize him," Juliette pointed out. "And maybe my being out there will flush him out..." Because this had to end soon. Pandora wanted to go home—to her bedroom with all its stuffed toys and to her familiar bed.

And to her daddy...

This morning she'd asked if he was going to come live with them when they went home. Blake had told her that was her and Mommy's house, not his. His home wasn't in Red Ridge anymore. Would he leave once the killer was caught?

Of course he would. His business was called Blake Colton International. Not Blake Colton Red Ridge, South Dakota. He would have to return to his headquarters in London or his other branches in Hong Kong and Singapore.

Her face flushed as she realized how well she'd kept apprised of him in the past. She told herself that it was just because he was Pandora's father. But Juliette had been keeping track of him even before that night they'd conceived their child.

She'd had a crush on Blake Colton for a long time.

But a crush was all it was. Nothing could ever come of it. They were too different. Her life was in Red Ridge as a K9 cop. His was in international cities with his business and his models and actresses.

She doubted he was going to give any of that up— even for his daughter. But she was worried that Pandora, after just that one meeting, had already gotten attached to her daddy. And Juliette was worried that after watching him during that meeting—watching him play and speak so sweetly with their little girl—that Juliette was getting too attached, as well.

"Walsh!" the chief shouted her name.

And she realized she'd missed whatever he'd been saying—to her. Her face flushed even hotter with embarrassment. "I'm sorry," she murmured. "What were you saying?"

"That you are not going to use yourself as bait to flush out this lunatic," the chief said. "That's too damn dangerous."

If he wasn't the boss, Juliette might have dared to call him a hypocrite. Not too long ago he'd used himself as bait to flush out the Groom Killer. He'd drawn out an obsessed stalker instead.

"I don't have to," she said. "I just need to do my job. He must be involved with the drug problem in Red Ridge since he killed that woman in the park to take that briefcase of drugs from her. My partner is the drug sniffing expert. I need to keep going to the train terminal and the airport and the bus terminal..."

The more people she caught smuggling drugs in and out of Red Ridge, the better the chance that she would get a lead on the killer during one of those arrests.

"You're going to have another patrol car on you at all times," the chief said.

She shook her head. "That's not necessary. We're already spread thin—with the Groom Killer on the loose."

"The killer hasn't acted in a while," the chief reminded them.

"About the same amount of time since anyone's heard from Demi..." Carson muttered. But his comment was loud enough for Brayden to overhear and tense with anger.

So much for the détente...

Then Carson shook his head and murmured an apology before adding more loudly, "Probably because everybody's scared to even think about getting married…"

But Juliette knew many of her coworkers were already thinking about it. Even the chief had recently fallen in love and moved in with the first murder victim's ex-wife, Darby Gage. And Juliette knew her best friend Elle Gage had fallen in love, as well—with a Colton, no less. Juliette suspected there were probably quite a few secret engagements in Red Ridge. She figured that was one secret that she and Blake would never have between them.

Unless he was already engaged to someone else— to one of those models or actresses he dated. But then, she would have already read about that in the tabloids.

No. He probably meant what he'd told her nearly five years ago about never wanting to get married. And she knew that she would not be the one to change his mind.

Blake had been quiet when they'd left the safe house with just enough time to spare so Juliette wouldn't miss the morning meeting. Maybe he'd just been tired since they had not slept at all the night before. She was tired. But she didn't think that was why he hadn't talked to her. It probably hadn't been because he had been worried that the bodyguards might have overheard their discussion, either.

She suspected he'd been angry. After meeting their amazing little girl and realizing what he'd missed, he was probably so furious with Juliette that he wouldn't care anymore if the killer got to her.

Because when she stepped out of the meeting, she didn't find him waiting in the hall for her. The only person in the reception area was Lorelei Wong. She glanced up from her desk and smiled at Juliette. Her silver-framed glasses had slipped down her nose. She pushed them up and blew a breath through her black bangs as she spoke on the phone.

She was too busy again to talk—probably fielding calls about the Groom Killer.

Juliette just waved at her as she and Sasha headed out to their patrol car. As she put the beagle in her harness in the back of the vehicle, she glanced around and still caught no sight of Blake. Of course, she hadn't noticed him the day before, either—until after work. So he might have been out there—with the bodyguards whose presence she didn't notice.

Despite the heat of the July day, she shivered. The killer could be out there and undetected, too. If he was smart, though, he'd be lying low—because he'd made a serious mistake when he'd shot a Red Ridge police officer. Now the entire department was even more determined to find him.

"Dad wants to see you," Patience told Blake.

"He knows where to find me," Blake reminded her. Even if he didn't own the hotel anymore—with all the financial difficulties he was currently having—he would know it was where Blake would stay.

"And I already told you that I can't help him," Blake reminded her. Withdrawing the amount of cash from his corporation that his father needed could cripple his business and cost too many of his loyal employees their jobs. He couldn't do it—not even to save Layla from marrying some old wealthy guy who'd struck a deal with Fenwick Colton. What he'd rather see was Layla standing up for herself, choosing her life and her heart over business. For once.

Patience's sigh rattled the cell phone Blake held. The rental car didn't have Bluetooth. After he'd brought back the damaged one, the company had been willing to loan him only one of their older models. He hoped it was reliable enough to follow Juliette's patrol car. Maybe he just needed to buy a vehicle—something like the SUVs the bodyguards he'd hired drove. Not that he could see them...

He could see the other patrol car, though, the one the chief had following Juliette. She must have been headed toward the bus terminal. That was better than the places she'd gone the day before.

"Dad wants to see you because he's worried about you," Patience said.

And Blake snorted in derision. "Yeah, right..."

Even if his father had, by some odd chance, heard that Blake was present at the shooting the night before, Blake doubted he would have been all that concerned about his safety. They'd barely spoken the past five years.

"I told you about this Groom Killer," Patience said.

"Yeah, that's why Dad can't marry off Layla to some old guy and save his company," Blake said.

Patience expelled another sigh that was clearly of exasperation. Blake wasn't certain if she was exasperated with him or with their father, though.

He tried to focus on their conversation. But it was

hard when he was watching Juliette at the same time. She was so damn beautiful—even in the drab Red Ridge Police Department uniform. She and the beagle moved with confidence through the crowd of people in the bus terminal.

"I'm sorry," he said. "Why would Dad be worried about me?" Had he heard about him and Juliette? About his grandchild? Maybe Blake did need to speak with his father. But he hesitated even to tell his sister.

"I don't know," Patience said. "I assured him that you were in no danger."

He flinched as he remembered the night before— the bullets hitting the rental car so close to where he'd been standing. If Juliette hadn't knocked him down, if she hadn't saved his life…

Had he even thanked her?

Everything had happened so quickly at the plant nursery that he didn't think he had. And then after…

The hospital and the safe house and meeting Pandora…

His heart contracted, affection for the little girl squeezing it. He'd been so overwhelmed after meeting her that he hadn't been able to think, much less talk to Juliette. He should have thanked her for how well she'd raised their daughter. But he hadn't been entirely able to let go of his anger with her, of his resentment over her keeping him from being part of his child's life.

"It's not like you're about to get married or anything," Patience continued.

Blake opened his mouth to laugh, but the chuckle stuck in his throat as he wondered, should he be? Then he wouldn't have to worry about Juliette keeping him away from Pandora anymore. But that was crazy. He didn't have to marry Juliette to make sure any of that happened. He could legally claim his child without legally tying himself to her mother—to her lying, secret-keeping mother.

"No," he said. "I'm not about to get married…" Especially not to a woman he couldn't trust. And no matter how well she'd raised their daughter, Blake could not trust Juliette. Five years ago she'd led him to believe she was someone she wasn't and then she'd kept a secret from him.

Kept Pandora from him…

"That's good," Patience said. "I don't want to have to worry about you, too." Like she worried about Layla marrying a man she didn't love and about their father losing what mattered most to him—his company. She was worried about Bea, too. Their sister loved the bridal shop she'd inherited from her grandmother.

Blake understood his sister's concerns. And he didn't want to add to them. He knew he needed to tell her that she was an aunt. But then he would also have to tell her that the little girl had witnessed a murder and was in danger.

"Nope, you don't have to worry about me," he said. And he clicked off the call to quickly make another.

The bodyguard picked up on the first ring. "Yes?"

"Any sign of him?" Blake asked.

"We didn't get a look at him last night," the bodyguard reminded him. "But there's no one suspicious-looking hanging around…"

Just as the man made the claim, Juliette's canine partner reacted to someone boarding a bus.

It would make sense that the killer would be trying to leave town right now.

Was it him?

He had been told to leave town—actually, to get the hell out of it. His head still rang with the way his current employer had shouted the order at him. "What the hell were you thinking—shooting a cop?"

Juliette Walsh was a cop. If he hadn't missed and struck the male officer instead, he would have *killed* a cop. But he hadn't bothered pointing that out.

"You've brought the heat of the entire department now," he'd been warned. "So you need to get the hell out of here!"

It was probably good advice. But he had unfinished business in Red Ridge. He had never left a witness alive before and he didn't intend to do that now. He had to find that little girl. He already knew where her mama was.

He also knew he wasn't the only killer in Red Ridge right now. "The police are all preoccupied with that Groom Killer," he reminded his boss. "I'm not their only focus."

"You are now," he'd been told. "No grooms have died lately. They probably think that killer's moved on. You need to do the same. Get the hell out of Red Ridge."

He'd reached for the back door to the realty company office. But a shout had stopped him. "And for God's sake, make sure nobody sees you leaving here!"

Anger twisted his guts. They'd begged him to come work for them. Luring him with the promise of big money for carrying out their dirty work. But now that his hands were dirty, they wanted nothing to do with him.

He was tempted to end not just his association with them but them, as well. He'd forced a smile instead.

"Nobody sees me come and go," he'd promised.

And the boss had snorted. "Except a little girl…"

He'd held on to his smile because he'd known that little girl would never be getting any bigger or any older than she currently was. Because she would soon be dead—right along with her cop mama…

# Chapter 9

Zane Godfried studied his face in the reflection of the rearview mirror of the Corvette his fiancée had given him as an engagement present. With his black hair slicked back and his teeth whitened to a brighter shade than his tuxedo shirt, he looked damn good—so good that it was a shame they had to keep this wedding on the down low. But it was the only way he had been able to convince Marnie Halloway to marry him.

Not that she hadn't wanted to. Since he'd connected online with the lonely, rich widow, she had been anxious to spend as much time as she could with him. First she'd sent him plane tickets to Red Ridge. Then she'd bought him his sweet ride. But when the whole Groom Killer crap had started, she'd been too worried about him to accept his proposal.

Fortunately for him, she was easily manipulated, and he'd been able to use those deaths as evidence that life was too short. More so for her than him. She was pushing seventy. He had to get her to do this now—before anyone figured out who Zane Godfried really was and where to find him.

He was in more danger from previous marks and loan sharks than he was from some serial killer. Of course, he didn't think it was really a serial killer on the loose. Wasn't it just some crazy broad who'd found out her baby daddy was going to marry someone else?

She'd killed him and then maybe a few more because she'd still been pissed. No more grooms had been killed lately, so she must have cooled off. Or left Red Ridge or the country.

Just like he'd told Marnie, nothing was going to happen to him. Though getting someone to perform their wedding ceremony hadn't been easy. He'd had to go online again to find somebody willing to do it. Fortunately for him again, pretty much anyone could get a license to marry people now, so he'd been able to find someone.

He glanced at the motel where the person had said for them to meet him. It looked a little seedy. Marnie probably wouldn't like this. Despite her age, she was acting like a blushing bride. The old chick probably had dementia, which was another reason Zane needed to push for this quickie wedding. He needed to clear out her bank accounts before someone figured out she'd lost her marbles.

And all her money…

He chuckled as he straightened his bow tie. Yeah, he

looked good. Who gave a crap what the motel looked like? He pushed open the driver's door and stepped into the parking lot.

It was early. So nobody was in the lot but him. Marnie was late. She was probably still trying to get beautiful. No matter how long she worked at that, it wasn't going to happen, though. He grimaced as he thought of his elderly bride. Then he looked again at the sexy red Corvette and smiled. At least he would have enough money to buy himself beautiful things. Like cars. And women...

A shadow reflected back from the side of the 'Vette as someone walked up behind him. He turned around, but instead of focusing on the person, he saw only the gun barrel pointed at him.

A shot fired, striking his chest with such force it knocked him back against the car. His last thought, as he slid down the side of it, was that he hoped he hadn't dented it. He didn't even get the chance to think that Marnie had been right; he was dead before he fully hit the ground.

Juliette stared at the body propped against the side of the Corvette. The pleated shirt, which had probably once been white, was stained red—with a gaping hole through the heart. And a black cummerbund spilled out between his open lips. His eyes stared up at them, glazed in death.

She resisted the urge to shudder. She should have been used to the sight by now. The Groom Killer had struck again.

"Who is he?" the chief asked as he joined them at the scene.

Detective Carson Gage had the guy's wallet, which he held out to his boss. "Your guess is as good as mine. He's got a few IDs in here."

"She says—" Juliette pointed toward the woman sitting in the back of an ambulance "—that his name is Zane Godfried." Juliette had been the first officer on the scene since the motel was near the train terminal where she and Sasha had been heading. She'd hoped to make more arrests like the one at the bus terminal.

She'd gotten that person only on a small amount of a controlled substance, though, which hadn't given her enough leverage to get him to talk about the killer from the park.

If he'd even known who he was…

He hadn't reacted when she'd described the killer to him.

"Marnie Halloway?" Finn asked as he peered into the ambulance.

Her makeup had run down and smeared her face. Some of it had even dripped onto the bodice of her white wedding gown.

"She met Godfried online a few months ago, and he convinced her to marry him," Carson said.

The detective had arrived soon after Juliette had—so soon that he'd probably been in the patrol car following her. Brayden Colton had been out riding with Carson, probably to prove to the chief that they were unified now.

Maybe something good had actually come of her

being in danger and Dean getting shot: the K9 unit had come back together as the family they'd always been before the Groom Killer had first struck Red Ridge.

She would have rather they'd put aside their differences and resentments without her daughter having to witness a murder and Dean having to take a bullet.

Carson and Brayden weren't the only ones who'd been following her, though. Blake had, too. He stood on the other side of the crime scene tape she'd strung up, around lamp posts in the parking lot, to keep out the reporters and morbidly curious gawkers who crowded all around Blake. Despite the crowd, he easily stood out. He was so damn handsome with his dark blond hair and those piercing green eyes.

"They were going to get married here?" the chief asked with a glance at the seedy motel. His brow furrowed as if he was confused.

Juliette shared his confusion. Marnie Holloway was a wealthy widow. She could have afforded a much more expensive venue. She could have—and probably should have—sprung for a destination wedding.

"The groom had found someone online who'd agreed to perform the ceremony," Carson said.

As chief, Finn had put out a warning weeks ago that nobody should attempt to get married until the killer was caught. Between sobs Marnie had said that she'd warned her groom it wasn't safe, but he'd been too eager to wait.

Probably too eager for her money.

"So this wedding was kept really hush-hush," the chief mused.

Juliette knew where he was headed with this—toward his cousin's innocence, although he'd done his best to appear impartial since that first murder. Bo Gage's.

"Demi couldn't have heard about their engagement," Juliette said for him. "It had to be someone right here in town." Someone watching and listening...

She shivered as she considered that idea—two killers out there now...

She was glad that Pandora was in the safe house with Elle protecting her. But the little girl wasn't the only person Juliette was worried about.

She glanced again at Blake. He had to stop following her around; it was too dangerous. His near miss at the plant nursery should have proved that to him. As she'd told him that night, he could have wound up in a body bag for real or, like Dean, in a hospital bed.

"It wasn't Demi," Brayden said, to Carson more than anyone else.

Carson looked like he was about argue, but then he just shrugged and turned away from Brayden. He called out to Dante Mancuso, who was guiding Flash around the parking lot, looking for evidence. "Any scent of..."

"Demi?" Brayden finished for him.

Dante didn't deny having Flash check for it. He just shook his head.

"That proves she hasn't been here," Brayden said. "Demi had nothing to do with this murder."

There had been evidence tying her to the other ones, though—evidence that not even her loyal brother had been able to explain. Of course, it could have been planted; he had raised that possibility.

"Demi knows dogs," Carson reminded him. "She knows how to get rid of or change her scent."

"That's a reach and you know it," Brayden said.

"We need to focus on this murder, this victim," Finn advised them. "Sounds like Godfried or whoever the hell he really is might have made some enemies of his own."

Carson nodded. "A person usually has a reason to use a bunch of different aliases. He or *she* either doesn't want to be found or caught…" He was obviously wondering if Demi Colton had changed her name. Maybe that was how she'd eluded all the people looking for her.

"We also need to have Katie check out all those identities of our victim," Finn said, referring to their tech whiz, Katie Parsons, "and see if he was ever romantically linked with Hayley Patton."

Was the chief beginning to suspect Hayley? Juliette wasn't a big fan of Bo Gage's *grieving* fiancée. They'd gone to the same school and Hayley had always treated Juliette like she was trash—even though they hadn't come from all that different backgrounds. Not like she and Blake had…

Just like she'd told Pandora, her daddy was a prince—or at least Red Ridge's equivalent of one. Her face heated with another rush of embarrassment that the little girl had shared that story with him. For that one night, when they'd created their daughter, Juliette had been his Cinderella. But unlike in the fairy tale, she and Blake were not going to wind up together.

He must have still been furious with her. He hadn't sought her out last night. He hadn't joined her when his bodyguards had slipped her into the safe house to tuck in Pandora for the night, either.

The little girl had asked about her daddy—had wondered where he was. From just that one meeting, she had gotten attached. Juliette never should have let them meet—not until she'd known how much a part of their daughter's life he wanted to be. She had a feeling that he didn't know that yet either, though.

"You all need to be extra careful out there," the chief cautioned the officers in the parking lot. He stepped closer and said to Juliette, "Especially you…"

She understood. Since the Groom Killer had struck again, the department would need to focus on finding that killer and not the one who had threatened her and Pandora.

"I'm glad now that Blake hired that security agency," Finn added.

She couldn't deny that they'd helped her—by getting her to see her daughter. But those visits were bittersweet because they were so short. She needed to be with Pandora again—home with her again.

She pointed to Blake. "You need to order him to back off."

"He's bothering you?" Finn asked.

Blake wasn't even talking to her. But Juliette nodded. "I can't worry about him while I'm watching out for the killer."

"Then maybe you need to go into that safe house with your daughter," the chief said.

How could he make such a suggestion when there

had just been another murder? Or maybe that was why he had.

But everyone else would be focused on finding the Groom Killer now, and the man who'd threatened Pandora could get away with murder. Maybe even theirs… if he managed to carry out that threat he'd made.

## Chapter 10

Blake hadn't slept for the past couple of nights, so he should have been exhausted. But every time he closed his eyes he saw that dead man, propped against the red Corvette with blood soaking his shirt and pooled all around him. And he also saw Dean Landon, the injured officer...

Blood oozing from his belly wound which was where one of the killer's bullets had struck him right beneath his vest. That injury had looked bad, too. Like it could have been fatal.

But that bullet had been intended for Juliette. The killer was out to get her and their child...

He shivered. But instead of pulling up his covers, he kicked them off. He couldn't stay in bed. He should be parked outside Juliette's house, making sure she was safe.

For Pandora's sake. The little girl could not lose her mother. Blake didn't want to lose her, either. Not that he had her…

He just didn't want anything bad to happen to her. But with the job she had, it was almost inevitable. As a police officer, she put herself in danger every day. And now, with the killer on the loose, she was in danger every minute of every day and night.

He jerked open a dresser drawer and reached for a pair of jeans. But before he could step into them, a knock rattled the door in the living area of the suite. He quickly pulled up the jeans and headed toward the door.

It was late. Who could be visiting him now?

Finn trying to once again talk him out of tailing Juliette? His cousin had tried that morning—at the crime scene. He'd said that Juliette was not appreciative of his constant presence. That Blake was more a distraction than a help…

He couldn't be any help in finding the killer. But he could be an extra set of eyes, so that she didn't get hurt trying to find the murderer. And for some reason, he just needed to be near her—to assure himself that she was all right.

He paused at the door, which rattled with another knock. He would be lucky if his visitor was Finn. It could be his dad or Patience at the door. He drew in a deep breath then pulled it open…and expelled that breath as if he'd been punched.

He'd expected anyone else at the door but her—but Juliette.

"Miss me?" he asked as he stepped back.

She walked in and slammed the door behind herself, then winced as she must have realized how loudly it had closed. Her face flushed, but then, her skin had already looked red when he'd opened the door to her. Maybe she'd gotten sunburned in the parking lot earlier that day.

But when he noticed she was glaring at him, he realized she was angry—really angry.

"What's wrong? What happened?" he asked.

She pointed her finger at him. "You are. You're what's wrong."

He shook his head. "You're wasting your time. Finn already talked to me today. And like I told him, I'm not backing off. I'm going to keep following you."

"To your death," she said.

"That's my choice," he said. "I'm a big boy. I know the risks."

"Death," she said. "That's what you're risking. You saw it today. Do you want to wind up like that murder victim? With a bullet through your heart?"

He wasn't worried about a bullet. He was worried about her. Their daughter needed her. He was also beginning to worry that he did, too. She was so damn beautiful that his blood pumped hot and fast through his veins. He wanted to be with her—badly.

Like they'd been together that night so long ago...

His lips curved into a grin, and he teased her, "I didn't know you cared so much about me."

Her eyes narrowed more in an angrier glare. "I don't care and apparently neither do you!"

His head was beginning to pound—from her yelling and from her confusing him. He was following her around—didn't he care too much?

"What are you talking about?" he asked.

"I'm talking about Pandora."

He sucked in a breath. "What about her? Is she okay?"

Juliette shook her head, tangling her blond hair around her face. When she was working she wore it in a ponytail. Otherwise it was down and loose around her shoulders like now.

Blake felt the silky strands of it when he grasped her shoulders. "What? What happened? Did he find the safe house?"

Maybe it hadn't been a good idea for her and him to visit the little girl. Maybe despite the bodyguards' best efforts, they had been followed.

"No," she said. "That's not the issue. Neither is the killer. *You're* the issue. *You* haven't found your way back to the house again."

He furrowed his brow as confusion rushed over him. "I don't understand…"

"And neither does Pandora," she said. "She doesn't understand why her *daddy* hasn't come back to see her. She doesn't understand why I'm the only one tucking her in at night."

Blake grimaced at the twinge in his heart. "I—I didn't think…"

She shrugged off his hands as if she couldn't bear to have him touching her. "No, you didn't think of Pandora—of how you could disappoint her."

"I thought of that," he said. "That's why I haven't

been back. I didn't want to disappoint her." Like his father had disappointed him so many times.

Even now…

Patience had claimed Fenwick wanted to see him, but he hadn't come by the hotel. He hadn't called. That was just Blake's sister's wishful thinking—that their father had enough heart to actually care about any of them.

And if his father didn't have enough heart, Blake wasn't sure that he did either.

"You disappointed her by not coming back," Juliette said. "She keeps asking me where you are…" Her voice cracked with emotion.

And Blake's heart felt like it cracked with regret. "I'm sorry. I didn't think she would care that much."

"For years she has asked me about her father," Juliette said.

"And you told her I was a prince," he said.

Her face flushed again, but this time it was definitely with embarrassment. Then she lifted her chin and replied, "Well, you are."

He snorted.

"You're the only male heir of Fenwick Colton," she said. "Doesn't that make you the prince of Red Ridge?"

"Hell, no," he said. "My father doesn't care about having a son or a daughter. He doesn't care about his kids at all or he wouldn't be trying to marry off one of my sisters to some rich old man to save Colton Energy."

"Is that why you came back to Red Ridge?" she asked.

He shrugged. "I don't know why I came back. I can't bail him out."

"Can't or won't?" she asked.

"Can't," he said. "Not without a lot of my employees losing their livelihoods." And he wouldn't do that to people who'd been loyal to him. "Fenwick will need to find another way to save his business—besides selling my sister Layla to the highest bidder." Which sounded pretty much like what he'd done.

"Fenwick Colton is Pandora's grandfather," she murmured, as if the fact had just occurred to her. She shuddered.

He reached out again, settling his hands on her shoulders to offer a reassuring squeeze. "You don't have to worry. I will never let him hurt her."

"I wish you could say the same about you," she said.

And that twinge struck his heart again. She'd made it clear that he had already hurt the little girl. He stepped back, dropping his hands from her shoulders. Then he ran one, which was shaking slightly, over his bed head tousled hair.

"That was the last thing I wanted to do…" he murmured. "That's why I stayed away the past couple of nights. I didn't want to screw this up…"

But he had. He turned and headed to the glass exterior wall that looked out over the glittering lights of the city below. There weren't many—not in comparison to his places in London, Hong Kong or Singapore. He was like his mother, too, and she hadn't known how to be a parent any more than his father had. "I don't know how to do this…"

"What?" she asked. And he saw her reflection in the glass as she walked up behind him. She was wearing another skirt. This one was a dark denim, and it was short—probably in deference to the heat. And probably also because of the heat, she wore a sleeveless blouse with it. She looked so damn beautiful—no matter what she wore.

He wanted to see her again in nothing at all. But she was too angry with him. And he was…

He reached for the resentment, trying to pull it up again. Trying to be angry with her for keeping him from his child. But the past couple of nights he'd kept himself from her.

He was scared.

"I don't know how to be a father," he said. "I don't know anything about kids—about how to talk to them or relate to them…"

"What!" she said again. But it sounded more like an exclamation than a question. And she grabbed his arms and spun him around to face her. "You were great with her that first time. That's why she misses you—that's why she wants to know everything about you. And she wants you to know everything about her…" She bit her lip now and tears pooled in her eyes.

And his heart lurched in his chest again. It wasn't just the child he'd hurt; he'd hurt the mother, too. "I'm sorry," he said again.

She shook her head. "I shouldn't be jealous, but I am. It's been just her and me all these years."

He felt that twinge again, and it must have shown in his face because she squeezed his arms.

"I'm sorry," she said. "I know that was selfish."

Selfish. Or selfless? He wasn't sure now. She'd already been struggling to pay off her mother's medical bills—according to Finn—and to put herself through college. And then she'd taken on the expense of raising a child alone. How the hell had she managed?

She was incredible.

"I'm so sorry I kept her from you," she continued. "I should have told you. I could have tracked you down through your family. I know that…" But her face flushed again with the embarrassment Blake knew that would have caused her.

And he honestly wasn't sure they would have believed her. He'd never talked about her, had never talked about that night. "I still need to tell them," he said.

She tensed. "You haven't?"

He shook his head. "I said before—I'm not close to my family…" And he was beginning to see maybe that was as much on him as on them. He'd even pulled back from his daughter just days after realizing he had one. He drew in a deep breath. "But I'll do better. I'll do better with Pandora."

She tilted her head and studied him, as if wondering if she should believe him.

Apparently he wasn't the only one struggling with trust.

"I don't want to hurt her," he said. "That's why I stayed away the past couple of nights."

"I was surprised," Juliette said. "You've been following me everywhere—but there. It seems like you would rather put yourself in danger than see your daughter."

She had no idea how dangerous seeing that little girl was for Blake. He wasn't just afraid of screwing up and hurting her. He was afraid of getting hurt. It was easier for him to risk his life than his heart.

"It's hard to see her," he said, "and think about what I missed."

She flinched now, and the tears that had glistened in her eyes spilled over, sliding down her cheeks. "I'm sorry. I can't give those years back to you."

She couldn't.

He would just have to accept that and let go of his anger. "Just like how you were jealous tonight when she asked about me," he said. "It's hard to see the two of you together—that bond you share. It's beautiful, but it's something I will never have with her."

"That's not true—"

"I'm a stranger she wants to get to know. You're the parent who was always there." And his voice cracked with emotion.

Juliette closed her eyes, but the tears kept sliding down her face. Her emotion moved him to put aside his resentment to comfort her. He pulled her into his arms and held her close.

She tilted her face up to his. "I'm sorry. I really am sorry…"

He slid his fingertips along the delicate line of her jaw. She was so beautiful, so fragile-looking, but that fragility was just an illusion. She was incredibly strong—to survive what she had with losing her mother at such a young age and to do the work that she did as a K9 officer.

"I know," he said. And he had to stop beating her up about it.

She couldn't change the past any more than he could.

He closed the short distance between their faces and brushed his mouth across hers. Her breath escaped in a sweet sigh across his lips. Then she kissed him back.

It was like that night so long ago in this very suite. The passion between them ignited, burning so hot. He'd never felt an attraction like this to anyone else—never before or since Juliette.

She ran her hands over his chest, and he realized he'd never put on a shirt. Her skin touched his, making him tingle—making him hard.

"I want you," he said, and his voice sounded so deep and gruff as desire nearly strangled him. Want didn't even seem adequate to describe the hunger burning inside him, making him ache.

She kissed him again with a hunger of her own, a hunger that almost matched his.

He groaned, and her tongue slid between his lips, mating with his. She tasted so damn sweet...

And she smelled like honeysuckle and sunshine, yet he didn't think it was just the shampoo. It was like it was her essence because he could taste the sweetness on her lips and feel the heat of her mouth.

She pulled back, gasping for breath, and murmured, "I want you..."

He swung her up his arms, like he had that night on the stairs. Like that night, she slid her arms around his neck, holding him as he held her. He turned toward the bedroom.

But as he turned, the door to the hall rattled. It wasn't

with a knock, though. It was just a faint noise as the handle jiggled.

Someone was at the door. Someone was trying to get in without alerting them to his presence. The officers or bodyguards wouldn't do that. Probably only the killer would. Just like that night at the plant nursery, he must have been following Juliette tonight.

He was going to try to kill her—right here.

# *Chapter 11*

Juliette had been so careful to make sure that she wasn't followed. She'd been certain she'd lost the killer and the bodyguards since neither could have been all that familiar with Red Ridge. She'd even lost the patrol car stationed outside her house because she hadn't wanted her coworkers to know where she was going—to see Blake.

She figured that they already suspected Pandora might be his child. So if they followed her to his hotel suite, they would have speculated that something was going on between them again.

And that wasn't why Juliette had come to him. Nothing had been going on between them. Well, clearly that had changed. She'd told herself she'd only come here to confront him about disappointing their daughter. But when he'd kissed her...

She'd forgotten about her anger. And she'd forgotten about that killer...

Until now. That had to be who was messing with the door, trying to get inside the suite undetected. She reached inside the bag slung over her shoulder and pulled out her service weapon. Sliding off the safety, she pointed the pistol toward the door.

Her instinct was to let him get inside the suite. Then it would be easier to apprehend him—even if she had to put another bullet in him to do that.

But Blake might get hurt...

She gestured at him to go into the bedroom and close that door. But he just shook his head. And then his cell phone rang. He must have had it in the pocket of his jeans because the bells pealed loudly, echoing in the living room.

The rattling at the door stopped.

"Damn it..." she murmured.

As he accepted the call, she headed toward the door. "The bodyguards are in the hotel, looking for the man they saw following you," Blake related. "Once they caught up to you."

She'd been so careful that she was surprised that they had. But they weren't the only ones. The killer had caught up to her, too.

Juliette knew where he was—or where he'd been. He couldn't have gotten far. Or he might not have left yet at all. She kept her back against the foyer wall as she neared the door. Then she reached out, jerked open the handle and swung her gun into the hall.

"Wait!" Blake called after her.

But she had already slipped into the corridor, once again keeping her back against the wall.

"Wait for them!" he called out.

"Stay here!" she yelled at him as she headed down the hall. She heard a door closing. At this hour, she didn't think it was a guest. And none of the elevators she passed were at the top floor, so it must have been to the stairwell at the end of the hall. She rushed toward it.

She had to catch him. She had to end this.

So she wasn't even thinking as she pushed open the door to the stairs. She wasn't thinking that he might have been standing behind it, waiting for her—until a big hand wrapped around her wrist and struck it against the top railing to the stairs.

Pain radiated up her arm. But she didn't loosen her grasp on her weapon. If she dropped it, then she had no chance of surviving. Even with his wounded shoulder, he was so much stronger than she was.

She couldn't lose her weapon.

But then his hand moved from her wrist to her shoulders, and he pushed—trying to send her over the railing and down twenty-one stories. Now she dropped the gun as she struggled to hold on to the railing. It clattered as it hit the stairs below her. But it didn't fire—fortunately.

As she tried to hang on, she looked up—and into those cold eyes of the killer. His hands moved from her shoulders to her throat. He squeezed, cutting off her breath, and his mouth curved into a cruel grin as he told her, "Your kid is next, bitch!"

Blake's heart stopped beating entirely as he pushed open the door to the stairwell. He'd been only seconds behind Juliette. But he was too late—just like the bodyguards would be when they made it up to the twenty-first floor. The killer had his hands on her—around her throat now—trying to choke the life out her.

Blake balled his hand into a fist and swung it at the guy. He caught him by surprise—enough that the guy loosened his grip. But so did Juliette, her hands sliding from the stairwell railing. Blake lunged for her, catching her. But he missed a few steps and slammed into the brick wall of the stairwell before regaining his footing.

"I'm going to make sure you stop playing her hero," the man said as he raised a gun, pointing the barrel down the stairwell—right at Blake.

Juliette had regained her footing, as well, and she grabbed Blake's hand—pulling him down the stairs. As they ran, shots rang out—the blasts echoing through the stairwell. Bullets struck the wall near their heads, sending chips of brick back at them.

One caught Blake's cheek, stinging. He ignored the pain and hurried along behind Juliette. But he collided with her as she stopped on a landing. Then she was moving around—back up the stairs.

Her gun gripped tightly in her hands, she began to fire back. Her shots were even louder, the blasts ringing in Blake's ears, and his head began to pound. While there had been shooting a couple of nights ago, he hadn't been this close—with his head nearly next to the weapon.

But then it stopped firing as Juliette emptied the clip. "Run!" she yelled at him as she fumbled inside the backpack-style purse swinging from her shoulder. She was probably looking for more ammunition.

Blake didn't move. He couldn't go without her. He couldn't leave her behind and unprotected.

She shoved at him, trying to get him out of the way as more shots rang out.

These were not hers. These were the killer's bullets coming at them—at him.

Finn had seriously just about had it with late-night visits and phone calls. Nothing good ever came of either. And this one was no exception. But this call had summoned him out of his house—to the Colton mansion on Bay Boulevard.

He drove past the Larsen twins' mansions, trying to peer beyond the gates. Despite the late hour, the homes were all lit up. Who the hell knew what was going on inside them? Parties? Clandestine meetings?

If only he could get some evidence that they were behind all the drugs coming in and out of Red Ridge…

But they were too smart for anything to stick. Finn had nothing but rumors and speculation, and no prosecutor could use those to convince a grand jury to indict. They were probably involved with that killer from the park, too, the one threatening Juliette and her daughter. He suspected that anything involving drugs in Red Ridge also involved them.

And that suitcase full of *sand* the little girl had seen the shooter take from the victim—that had to have been drugs. Once they'd ID'd the young woman, they'd found her prior arrest for some low-level dealing. Had the woman stolen the drugs and been trying to resell them? Had the killer murdered her to reclaim the drugs or to send a message to other dealers?

Whether intended or not, that message had been received, because no one was talking. Finn sighed as he drove past those mansions.

He had nothing on the Larsons. Yet. But hopefully that would change soon.

He also had nothing on the Groom Killer. That was what he'd already told Fenwick Colton when the man had called him. But the mayor of Red Ridge had insisted that Finn come out to his estate anyway.

The gates were open, so he drove right through and around the circular drive to the front door. Like the Larsons' mansions, this one was all lit up.

Didn't rich people sleep?

But then, it wasn't as if they had to punch clocks like working stiffs.

Finn shut off the ignition and headed up the walk to the front door. Fenwick must have been watching for him because the tall mahogany door opened before Finn could even ring the bell. "You took your time," the older man remarked.

And Finn grimaced. No thank you for agreeing to this late-night visit. No appreciation at all. Fenwick Colton had always been a loud blowhard. Rich and entitled. But he was even worse now than he'd been before—because now he was desperate.

Finn could see it in his eyes. They were glassy, too, as if he'd been drinking. It probably didn't take much for a guy as short and skinny as Fenwick to have had too much, though. The man turned from the door and walked away, expecting Finn to follow. And of course he headed, albeit a bit wobbly, to the den and straight to the bar in the corner of it.

"Drink?" he asked as he lifted a decanter of liquor.

Finn shook his head.

"So you're on duty?"

"No," Finn said. "I told you that when you called. I was home in bed." With the most beautiful woman… and once again he'd had to leave her. He'd known being police chief was a full-time job, but with the Groom Killer on the loose, it had become an around-the-clock position.

"How can you sleep with what's happening in Red Ridge?" Fenwick asked, his face tight with disapproval. "Killers on the loose, spoiling weddings."

Once Katie Parsons had dug up more on the latest murder victim, Finn wasn't so sure that the killer hadn't actually done Marnie Halloway a favor. Neither Zane Godfried nor any of his other aliases had been a good person. Marnie was probably better off that the wedding had never happened.

But as someone who longed to get married himself, Finn was frustrated that they had yet to catch the Groom Killer.

"You need to step up your efforts to track down Demi Colton," Fenwick told him.

It wasn't the first time the businessman had told Finn how to do his job. Even if Fenwick wasn't also the mayor of Red Ridge, Finn suspected he still would have tried steering this particular investigation. "Finding Demi is not our only concern right now," Finn said.

Especially when Finn wasn't even sure she had anything to do with the Groom Killer except for having once been involved with the very first victim. She couldn't have even known about the last one since the FBI had reported sightings of her far from Red Ridge. So how would she have had anything to do with his murder?

His path had never crossed Hayley Patton's, either. So that hunch Finn had started having about the first victim's fiancée hadn't panned out. He didn't necessarily think she was guilty—just someone involved, however indirectly, with the murders.

Fenwick waved a hand dismissively and said, "I hope you're not wasting your limited resources on finding a drug dealer's killer."

The mayor, once again, seemed to already be apprised of everything happening within the department.

"How'd you know she was a dealer?" Finn asked.

Fenwick winked. "I have my sources…"

Lorelei?

The receptionist was fiercely loyal, though. Finn doubted the mayor could have charmed her. But there were plenty of other people within the department who could have told him.

"It doesn't matter what the young woman was doing," Finn said. "She didn't deserve to die."

Fenwick snorted. "She knew the dangers. That kind of stuff happens all the time with their kind shooting each other over disputes."

"That killer also shot one of my officers and is trying to kill another one, as well as her daughter, who witnessed that murder." Her daughter. *Your granddaughter.*

It wasn't Finn's place to tell Fenwick Colton that he was a grandpa—although he would love to see the vain playboy's face when he heard the news. And that was news he must not have heard yet or he wouldn't have been so quick to dismiss the importance of finding the man who'd threatened his granddaughter.

Fenwick shrugged. "The Groom Killer still needs to be your top priority."

"Finding the guy shooting and threatening my officers is my top priority," he said. He hated that he'd come so close to nearly losing one of them. He didn't want that to happen again—with Juliette Walsh.

"You need to remember, Finn," the mayor persisted, "that if Layla can't get married and save my company, your resources will be even more limited."

Finn flinched—even though it wasn't the first time he'd heard the threat. He knew where Fenwick was heading with this.

"I subsidize the K9 program per my late wife's wishes," the older man continued. "But I won't be able to afford to do that much longer…"

Finn had nothing to do with business, so he didn't know how Fenwick had gotten into his current predicament. He also didn't know how a man could barter one of his children's lives as a way to get out of it.

And now he realized why Blake hadn't told his father that he had a granddaughter. Hell, if Finn had a daughter, he wouldn't want Fenwick Colton to know it, either.

Before he could even decide if or how he wanted to reply, his cell phone vibrated in his pocket. He pulled it out, which caused Fenwick to grumble at the rudeness. Ignoring him, he accepted the call, "Chief Colton…"

"Chief, it's Frank," the dispatcher said. And he sounded nearly as upset as he had the night Finn had had an officer down.

"What is it?" Finn asked, as his heart pounded heavy and hard with dread. "Not…"

"There's been a shooting at the Colton Plaza Hotel," Frank replied.

"Any casualties?"

"Not that have been reported," Frank replied. "But it is officer-involved."

"Which officer?" he asked this time.

Last time he'd made an assumption and he'd been wrong. But it had been a safe assumption to make since he had only one officer a murderer was determined to kill.

"Juliette Walsh," Frank confirmed.

"Was she alone?"

"No," Frank replied. "Blake Colton is with her."

Finn flinched. "I'll be right there." He clicked off the call and slid the cell into his pocket. But he hesitated before turning toward the older man.

Had Fenwick overheard any of the conversation?

Did he know that his son had been involved in a

shooting? And while there had been no reports of casualties yet, that didn't mean that there wasn't one.

Or two…

## Chapter 12

"Where the hell did he go…?" Juliette murmured as she followed Sasha around the perimeter of the hotel. Animals were not allowed in the hotel, so she'd left Sasha in the car when she'd arrived. Despite being July, the evening was cool. So Sasha had been fine with the windows down and a bowl of fresh water on the back seat with her. Juliette hadn't intended to stay longer than the time it would have taken to give Blake a piece of her mind over not seeing their daughter again. But then he'd kissed her…

If not for the killer interrupting them, they would have done more than that. So it was probably good that he'd interrupted them. But trying to kill them…

Fortunately the bodyguards had shown up in the stairwell and the killer had fled out a door on another story. The bodyguards had then moved to cover all the exits—to catch him when he tried to escape.

But they hadn't seen anyone leaving the hotel. Not even a guest or employee.

It was in the middle of shift, so an employee wouldn't have been leaving. And it was so late that guests were probably already settled in for the night.

While she and Sasha were checking the perimeter, Dante Mancuso and Flash were inside—trying to track the killer to a room. The man had nearly opened the door to Blake's suite, so he might have been able to open another one and slip inside to hide.

Once she'd slid in another clip and started firing back at him, he'd taken off onto a floor above where she and Blake had been.

Blake...

He was okay—but for a scratch on his face. He'd claimed that wasn't because of a bullet directly but from a bullet breaking off brick that had struck his face.

His handsome face...

He'd looked so worried when she'd insisted on retrieving Sasha from her car to search the lot. He'd been concerned about her.

She was worried about him. He was the one still in the hotel and, unless the bodyguards had missed him exiting, so was the killer.

But Flash was the best tracker in Red Ridge. If the killer was inside the hotel, he and Dante would find him. And Blake was not alone in his suite. The chief was inside with him.

And so was his father...

The mayor of Red Ridge hadn't even acknowledged her when she'd walked past him. It had reminded her of how Blake had walked past her that morning after their incredible evening together. Because she'd been dressed as a maid, he hadn't even noticed her. No. She would never be a Colton—never be Blake's Cinderella. But the truth was that she had given birth to a Colton.

Would her grandfather accept Pandora? Or would he ignore her like Blake claimed the man had ignored his own children? Maybe that would be best for the little girl, though.

"Find anything?" Dante Mancuso asked through the radio Juliette held.

She pressed down the button. "No. You?"

"No."

She wasn't surprised at his response—not after his asking her. "Nothing?"

"Flash tracked him from the stairwell to the corridor of the eighteenth floor. He walked down it to a service elevator. We stopped on every floor to see which one he got out on," Mancuso wearily continued. "He appears to have taken it to the basement."

"So he must still be down there," she said hopefully, and she turned back toward the building. "Blake's body-guards were on the exits and didn't see him leave."

She suspected they were watching her now, though, so the killer could have slipped out of the basement recently. She hoped like hell he hadn't, though. She wanted to catch him so badly—for terrorizing her daughter and for shooting at Blake and injuring her coworker. Not to mention murdering that woman in the playground parking lot.

He had to be stopped before he hurt anyone else.

Mancuso's voice emanated from the radio. "I don't think he's here. Flash just stopped at some kind of manhole in the floor—it looks like it goes into the sewer."

So he'd made it out.

And he could be anywhere in Red Ridge by now.

Despite the warmth of the July night, Juliette shivered at the thought of the killer still being on the loose. She had no doubt he hadn't gone far, though. He was too determined to carry out his threat to kill her and Pandora.

Frustration gripped Blake. He did not have time for this—for whatever the hell this ambush was with Finn bringing his father to his hotel suite.

Finn pointed toward Blake's face. "You should get that checked out."

"I told you I did not get shot." He'd told Juliette the same thing when she'd noticed the cut and had been concerned. She'd also been angry with him, though. Angry like the chief and his father were—for putting himself in danger.

But if he hadn't chased her down the hallway, if he hadn't intervened in the stairwell…she would have been dead or at least severely wounded.

Anger surged through him now. He needed to be talking to the security agency he'd hired—not Finn and definitely not his father. While they had intervened and saved them in the stairwell, they'd still let the killer get away. And earlier that evening, they'd let Juliette slip away from them. Sure, they'd found her, but unfortunately, the killer had found her first.

His father hadn't actually said a word yet, though. He just looked angry—his face pinched and flushed. But then the words he must have been holding back finally burst free. "You're damn lucky you didn't get shot—what with all the bullets flying around the hotel. I heard all the guests complaining about the ruckus."

That was it. His father was worried about the Colton Plaza Hotel—not his son. Probably concerned that he'd have to refund money to those complaining guests.

"Don't worry, Dad," Blake replied, his voice sharp with bitterness. "There was no real damage—just a few chips out of the brick wall in the stairwell."

He touched his cheek again and winced at the sting of it. A few crumbs of that concrete were embedded in his skin. He probably should head to the ER. But first he wanted to check on Juliette.

She'd sworn she was fine. But how could she be after that close call?

Blake was still shaking—not with fear but with adrenaline. It coursed through him, making his pulse race and sweat trickle down between his shoulder blades. He'd pulled on a shirt when he'd returned to his suite, which was probably good so nobody had noticed he had a few more scratches on his back and chest from those concrete chips.

But he would be fine.

The killer hadn't really been aiming for him. Juliette

had been his target. She was the one in danger. She and their daughter.

"I'm not worried about the damn hotel!" Fenwick replied. But his face had flushed an even brighter shade of red and Blake knew he'd touched a nerve. The old man cared about the business—hell, it was all he'd ever cared about. "I'm worried about you!"

Blake glanced at Finn now and narrowed his eyes. What had the police chief told his father?

Everything?

Anything?

As if he'd read his mind, Finn shook his head.

And the pressure in Blake's chest eased slightly. But maybe it would have been easier if Finn had told the old man and spared Blake the scene he anticipated.

He assured his father, "You don't need to worry about me."

Fenwick gestured at Blake's face, and his hand was shaking. "You could have been killed."

"By a concrete chip?" Blake snorted. "Not likely."

"By a bullet. Someone was shooting at you. Why was someone shooting at you?"

"He wasn't shooting at me," Blake said.

"He just got in the way," Finn added, and there was bitterness in his voice. "That's why I didn't want you following her around. I knew you were going to get your head blown off and it damn near happened!"

"Who?" Fenwick asked. But his question was for the police chief now as if he didn't trust Blake to answer him. "Who is he following around?"

Finn glanced at Blake and raised his eyebrows. "You want me to answer him or are you going to do it?"

"Who?" Fenwick asked, and he turned to Blake now.

Blake wasn't sure how to answer his father. What was Juliette? A one-night stand? His old lover? If the killer hadn't interrupted them, she would have been his lover again.

Whatever else she was to Blake, she was the mother of his child.

"Who?" Fenwick asked impatiently, and he'd turned back to Finn again.

"One of my officers," Finn replied. "The one whose life is in danger."

Fenwick sucked in a breath. His brow furrowed, he focused on Blake again. "Why are you getting involved in this? You've only been back in town a few days."

It had been longer than that, but Blake wasn't about to point out that he'd been home a while and hadn't contacted his father. The man was already angry and confused enough.

Which struck Blake as odd...

Could the old man care more than he'd realized?

"You can't know this woman," his father continued. "She's just some cop..."

Nope. His father hadn't changed. He was still an entitled snob. That was what Juliette had thought he was all those years ago when he'd walked past her in her maid's uniform and hadn't even noticed her. How could he have done that?

Was he his old man's son? A rich and entitled snob?

"She's the mother of my child," Blake said. "The mother of your grandchild."

Fenwick's eyes nearly bugged out of their sockets. "What? What the hell did you just say?"

Finn headed toward the door. Blake gestured him back. But Finn shook his head and quietly murmured, "This is a private family matter."

Finn was family, too. Blake was probably closer to his cousin than he was any of his sisters or his dad. And he hadn't seen his mom in years, either, since she was always traveling.

He glared as the police chief headed out the door. Before it closed, Blake mouthed the word, "Coward" at him. Finn grinned as he shut the door.

Silence fell over the room for a long moment while Fenwick digested the news.

But just in case he hadn't understood, Blake rubbed it in. "You're a grandpa."

That would probably kill his vain father. The guy wore a blond toupee to hide his thinning hair and dated women Blake's age rather than his own. He was desperately trying to appear younger than he was.

"I want to see her," Fenwick said.

Blake shook his head. "Nope."

"*If* she's my granddaughter," he said with suspicion, "I have the right to see her."

Blake sighed. Of course, his father would think to question paternity. "As long as I'm yours, she's your granddaughter." That dimple in her left cheek was DNA enough to prove it to him.

"Don't be naive," his father admonished him. "A lot of women would like to have a Colton heir."

Blake snorted now. "Her mother didn't even tell me about her. If she wanted a Colton heir, she would have told me she'd borne one before now."

"How old is this kid?" his father asked, his voice still sharp with suspicion.

His little girl wasn't just *this kid*.

"Pandora," Blake told him her name. "And she's four."

"You left five years ago."

"Not quite five yet, and the timing is right," he said.

But his father's eyes were narrowed in skepticism. He probably really did not want to be a grandfather. Or he thought Blake was a fool.

"Why can't I see her?" he asked.

"She's in danger," Blake said, and he touched his cheek again and shuddered at the thought of the little girl getting hurt. "She witnessed a murder, and the murderer wants to kill her."

Fenwick sucked in a breath. "And she's only four …?"

"She's too young to have seen what she did," Blake said. After visiting that crime scene in the parking lot, he understood more about what his daughter had witnessed. He'd only seen the aftermath, though—the death. She had seen the actual murder as it had taken place.

"Where is she?" his father asked.

"A safe house."

"I can't go to this safe house?"

Blake shook his head. "No. It's too risky." He could have had the bodyguards smuggle in his father like they smuggled in Juliette. But his father had never been good at sneaking around—that was why he'd been divorced three times.

"Is that the only reason you don't want me to see her?" Fenwick asked, and now he was suspicious of Blake.

Here was his chance to lobby for his sister. "With what you're doing to Layla—forcing her to marry a man she doesn't love to save your business..." He shuddered. "I'm not sure I want you anywhere near my daughter."

Fenwick's face flushed bright red now. "How dare you speak to me this way!"

And this was why Blake hadn't sought out his father when he'd returned to Red Ridge—because usually every conversation between them dissolved into a shouting match.

"I don't have time for this," Blake said. And he grabbed the keys for his rental car and headed toward the door.

"You're not going anywhere!" Fenwick yelled at him.

But Blake just kept walking—right out the door. He didn't have time to waste arguing with his father. He needed to check on Juliette. To make sure she was really okay and that she was safe...

But he had a horrible feeling that until the killer was caught, she wouldn't be safe—no matter how many people were trying to protect her.

The killer was too damned determined.

Fenwick gasped as the door slammed closed behind his son. He'd just walked away. Last time Blake had done that, he'd stayed away for five years. Fenwick shouldn't have been surprised that he had, though. Blake had always been his own man—even when he was just a little boy.

He was headstrong and stubborn.

And Fenwick worried those traits just might get him killed. He was determined to protect this woman— some old girlfriend—and a child that he didn't even have proof was actually his.

Why hadn't he demanded a paternity test the second she had made the claim? He was probably being taken advantage of…

And it wasn't just his money he was risking for her and this kid. He was risking his life for them, as well.

"Damn fool…" Fenwick murmured, his eyes stinging.

What if that had been the last time he saw his son?

# *Chapter 13*

Juliette stared at the clock beside her bed. If she closed her eyes now, she would get a couple of hours of sleep before the alarm went off.

If she could sleep…

But she closed her eyes, and nothing happened. She was too wired, her pulse still pounding, her blood still rushing quickly through her veins…

She had been so close…

To dying.

If Blake hadn't charged into the stairwell when he had, the killer would have thrown her down those twenty-one stories. She'd been losing her grasp on the railing and on her breath as he'd closed his hands around her throat.

But she'd lost something before that…when she'd

nearly made love with Blake. She'd lost control of the attraction she felt for him. It was even stronger now than it had been five years ago.

Maybe that was why her pulse kept pounding—because of the excitement of those kisses, the heat of the passion...

She kicked off her sheet and uttered a groan of frustration. It was no use. She was not going to sleep. But maybe that was a good thing, because she was awake enough to hear the creak of the floorboards of her front porch as someone headed toward her door.

Juliette was ready. She picked up her weapon next to her alarm clock. After flicking off the safety, she rolled out of bed. Her house was small—so small that it was just a few steps from her bedroom to the living room.

A knock sounded at the front door now. Maybe the killer had decided to forego trying to pick the lock. But then a voice called out, "Open up, Juliette. It's me."

Her pulse quickened even more than it had already been pounding as she recognized the deep voice. Blake.

Was that why Sasha hadn't joined her at the door? The beagle had been exhausted when they'd come home. She was also missing Pandora and had gone into the little girl's room and crawled onto her bed. The bodyguards and patrol officers must have realized it was him, too, since they'd let him get to the front door.

She hesitated a moment before reaching for the lock. And he knocked again.

"Come on," he said. "I doubt you're sleeping."

She turned the deadbolt and opened the door. "Who

can sleep with all the noise you're making out here?" she asked.

Hopefully he had not awakened her neighbors. Mrs. Ludwick might come over wielding her rolling pin as a weapon. While the rolling pin might hurt Blake, it would be no protection against the killer's gun.

Maybe she shouldn't have insisted on staying in her home. It wasn't just herself she was putting in danger but maybe her neighbors, as well. Of course the patrol car was parked out front, though—watching. And the bodyguards were somewhere…

The killer wouldn't try for her here.

"What the hell are you doing here?" Blake asked as he stepped through the door. "Are you trying to get killed?"

"No," she said. "That's what you do—when you keep putting yourself in danger."

He glared at her and sarcastically remarked, "You're welcome."

Heat rushed to her face. She hadn't thanked him yet. She'd just remembered that. "You did save me tonight," she said. "If you hadn't stopped him…" She shuddered. "He would have pushed me down the stairs. I didn't thank you then."

"You didn't have time," Blake said. "And I'm not here looking for gratitude. I'm here to point out that you nearly died tonight and then you come back here alone."

"Thanks to you and the chief, I'm never alone," she said. "You have bodyguards on me. And he has a patrol car following me around."

"And you still nearly got killed tonight," he pointed

out. "You're still not safe." He glanced around the house and gestured toward the big picture window in the living room. "Especially not here."

With all the backup she had at the moment, she wasn't concerned. After tonight, she'd learned to not try to lose them again. She also didn't think that the killer would risk another attempt on her life right now. He would know she had extra protection. She was actually surprised that Blake had gotten past everybody. But then, the bodyguards worked for him. And the police officers—her friends—must have realized that there was something going on between her and Blake.

"Then leave," she said. "If you don't feel safe here."

"I don't," he said. But he was staring at her so intensely—like she was the threat—not the maniac who'd shot at them in the stairwell.

"You claimed the bodyguards you hired are the best," she reminded him.

"They are, as long as you don't purposely try to lose them," he said. "But I'm not worried about the killer trying to shoot you again right now."

Probably because he'd read his security firm the riot act for letting the killer nearly get to her tonight. But that had been her fault. She'd tried really hard to lose them and the patrol car when she'd left her house earlier to confront Blake over disappointing their daughter. She hadn't wanted anyone to know that she was going to see him.

"So what are you worried about?" she asked.

"You getting to me," he replied. And he stepped

closer to her, his chest nearly brushing against her breasts.

Because of the heat and her temperamental air conditioner, she wore a light nightgown with thin spaghetti straps. The material was so thin that she could feel the heat of his body through it, and her nipples tightened and pushed against it.

Blake lifted his hand to her face. As he cupped her cheek in his palm, he ran his thumb across her mouth. "You are so beautiful…"

Her lips tingled from the contact with his skin. Her breath stuck in her throat. She wanted him to kiss her. She wanted him to touch her.

She glanced at the door and tilted her head to listen intently. Was anyone going to interrupt this time?

Nothing moved. There was no sound but the pounding of her own heart.

Then he slid his thumb from her lip and leaned forward—pressing his mouth against hers. The kiss was gentle at first then deepened with his groan. She delved into his hair with her fingers, clutching his head to hers as their mouths mated. Their lips nibbled at each other's, clinging in hungry kisses.

She didn't want to stop—knew they couldn't stop—even if the killer showed up at the door again. So she grasped his shirt and walked backward, tugging him along with her toward her bedroom. They didn't stop kissing, didn't even look to see where they were going. But they made it through the door and to the bed. When her legs hit the edge of the mattress, she tumbled down onto it, and Blake tumbled with her, sprawled across her.

She giggled. And he chuckled. Then he moved his weight off her, and she murmured a protest as she reached for him. She caught the waistband of his jeans. They were buttoned now, unlike when she'd shown up at the hotel and they'd been riding low on his lean hips. And he'd worn no shirt. He'd looked so damn sexy. Then.

And now.

His dark blond hair was tousled, and his green eyes were dark with desire as he stared down at her.

She unbuttoned his jeans and reached for his zipper. But he caught her hand in his and held it. His chest expanded with his sharp pants for air.

"You're driving me crazy..." he murmured.

"I haven't done anything..." Yet. But she intended to make love to him—like they had that night—like they were the only two people in the world. She knew they weren't, but she needed this moment—needed to escape from all the fear and stress overwhelming her.

Then he overwhelmed her—with his touch, his kisses...

As he pressed his mouth to hers, he trailed his fingertips down her shoulders, pushing the straps and the front of her nightgown down. Then he traced her collarbone before moving his hands to the swell of her breasts, cupping them in his hands and brushing his thumbs across the nipples.

She squirmed and moaned as heat streaked through her, from her breasts to her core. She pressed her legs together as she began to throb inside—where she wanted him to be.

With his hands busy on her body, she was able to tug down his zipper and free him. Her fingers slid over the erection straining against his knit boxers.

He groaned and pressed against her hand. And she knew he needed her as much as she needed him. But he pulled away from her to move down her body. He kissed her shoulder and the swell of her breast before closing his lips around one of her nipples. He tugged gently on it, and she arched off the bed.

"Blake!" she called as pleasure coursed through her. It wasn't enough, though. She was still full of tension, still full of desire and need.

She pulled on his shirt, dragging it up and over his head. He let her pull it off. But he didn't move back up. Instead he moved lower, and as he did, he slipped off her nightgown and tossed it onto the floor. Then he made love to her with his mouth.

She cried out as pleasure overwhelmed her. But still it wasn't enough…

When had she gotten so damn greedy?

Maybe it was because she knew that he could give her more pleasure than even that, than anyone else ever could…

She clutched at his bare shoulders, trying to pull him up. Instead, he got off the bed entirely.

Was he leaving her?

Was that all he intended to do? Give her pleasure yet take none for himself?

But he'd only stood to push off his jeans and boxers. Then he pulled a condom from a pocket of his jeans and rolled it over his shaft. He joined her on the bed, but he didn't immediately join their bodies. Instead he held his weight off her, their naked bodies just brushing against each other, as he kissed her. Tenderly…

Almost reverently…

Then the passion between them ignited, burning so hot that Juliette's skin heated. She reached up and locked her arms around his neck and her legs around his waist, pulling him down on top of her.

And finally he joined their bodies, easing inside her. She shifted and arched, taking him deeper. Then he began to move, and she bit her lip as the tension and the pleasure intensified. Each thrust brought her closer and closer to the edge of madness. She clutched harder at his back, his muscles rippling beneath her fingers.

She met each thrust, rising up from the mattress—pushing her hips against him. The tension spiraled inside her—out of control—until it finally broke. Her body shuddered, her inner muscles clenching and rippling as the orgasm overwhelmed her. She screamed his name.

Then he tensed and uttered a deep, almost guttural groan of pleasure. He leaned his head down, against her shoulder, as he panted for breath.

She was panting, too. She'd never felt anything as powerful—not even with him.

Finally he moved again, trying to ease out of her. But she clutched him, not wanting him to pull away. He felt so good—so perfect—inside her. As if they'd been made for each other…

But they had no more in common now than they'd had five years ago, except for their daughter. Pandora was the only bond they shared. Their lives were too different, were even in different countries.

She had to remind herself of that—he was only home for a visit. He wasn't staying. So she could not get attached—or let Pandora get too attached—because they would both wind up with their hearts broken.

Blake opened his eyes, then squeezed them shut again as the sunlight pouring through Juliette's bedroom window blinded him. He reached across the tangled sheets, looking for her, but the sheets were empty and probably warm only from the sunlight streaming through that window.

How long had she been gone?

How long had he been asleep?

He opened his eyes again, squinting, and peered at the clock beside the bed. It was nearly noon. All those sleepless nights must have finally caught up with him.

But where was Juliette?

He listened but heard no movement inside the house—just the sound of birds chirping outside the bedroom window. She was gone.

To work, probably.

At least the bodyguards he'd hired and some of her coworkers would be following her—because Blake was making a piss-poor protector.

But then, he wasn't a bodyguard. He was a businessman. He'd proved that last night. While he'd saved her from the killer pushing her down the stairs, he hadn't been able to catch the guy.

Neither had the bodyguards or the police officers,

though. So he probably wouldn't have felt too bad about his efforts to protect her—if Juliette hadn't managed to sneak away from him while they'd been sleeping in the same bed. He needed to be more alert to keep her safe.

Maybe she hadn't slept, though. He couldn't remember much after they'd made love...the third time...

They hadn't been able to get enough of each other—just like that night nearly five years ago. That night had had a once-in-a-lifetime feel to it, though—like it was just a stolen moment they'd needed to make the most of. Blake had already known then that he was going to leave Red Ridge. That the only way he could truly make it on his own was if he was somewhere that being a Colton didn't matter.

Maybe that was why he hadn't noticed her in her maid's uniform. He hadn't wanted to see her—hadn't wanted to have to say goodbye.

Was that why Juliette had slipped away from him today—just as she had after that night so long ago? She didn't want to say goodbye?

He could understand that five years ago. She'd been all hung up on the fact that she was a maid and he was the son of a millionaire. She'd thought they had nothing in common. And they hadn't.

They still didn't. Following her around the past few days had proved that to Blake. He was nowhere near as tough and brave as she was. He had no interest in risking his life day after day to serve and protect Red Ridge.

And Juliette was risking her life even more because there was a man on the loose determined to kill her. She should have woken him up—should have said goodbye—because Blake worried that she might not have the chance if the killer got her before he saw her again.

## Chapter 14

Sometimes Juliette wondered which of them was the handler. She or Sasha?

The beagle was the one leading her around the bus terminal. After another sleepless night, Juliette was too distracted to focus on the job. It might not have been lack of sleep that was distracting her, though, but thoughts of what she'd done with Blake Colton.

What the hell had she been thinking?

She hadn't been thinking. She'd just been feeling—so much passion for him. But if it had only been desire, she might not have been worried. Her feelings for Blake went deeper than lust, though.

Gratitude…

Not just for saving her life the night before but for giving her Pandora, as well. Their daughter was the greatest gift Juliette had ever received. At the time she'd learned she was pregnant, she'd been scared and overwhelmed.

But now…

She couldn't imagine her life without her child in it. Couldn't imagine not having Pandora to hold. Or seeing her smile.

Just as Mama had said, there was a reason for everything. Pandora was the reason for everything Juliette did now.

She needed to find this killer and put him in jail. She needed her child and her life back. That life hadn't included Blake.

Would it?

She doubted he would stay in Red Ridge, but would he come back more often to see his daughter? Or once he left, would they be out of his sight, out of his mind?

That must have been the case last time. He couldn't have looked for her very long before he'd left Red Ridge. And he had never come back to look for her again within those five years. That night—and she—had not meant as much to him as it and he had to her.

She was glad she'd slipped out of bed without awakening him. It would have been even more distracting had he been following her around today.

Sasha emitted a sound deep in her throat, and her hair began to rise on her neck. She'd caught the scent of something…

She'd also caught Juliette's attention. She shook her head, shaking off the sleepiness and distraction. She had to be focused now. Her life depended on it.

"What do you smell, girl?" Juliette asked.

And the white-and-brown dog turned back and looked at Juliette, as if asking if she was new. What the hell did Juliette think Sasha smelled?

Of course it was drugs. Sniffing them out was Sasha's specialty.

The beagle had found that small amount of marijuana on someone a few days ago. But this seemed bigger—Sasha seemed more excited, her little body trembling with it.

Juliette and Sasha weren't the only K9 team at the bus terminal. Carson Gage walked around the lines of people waiting outside for buses, as well. His German shepherd, Justice, was more a tracker than a drug sniffing dog, though.

She could have used them last night to find the killer. But once he'd disappeared into the sewer, probably not even Justice would have been able to track where he'd gone after that.

To her house?

Had he been watching her place last night? Waiting for another chance to shoot at her?

She shivered despite the afternoon heat.

Then Sasha stopped moving down the row and sat down next to the suitcase of a woman in line for the bus to Spearfish. The young woman dropped the handle of the small case and stared straight ahead, apparently trying to pretend that she was unaware of Juliette and the canine. Sweat beaded on the woman's brow and upper lip. She was young—with several tattoos covering her skinny arms. Her hair had been dyed purple but black roots showed at her scalp.

She looked familiar to Juliette. But then, she'd spent the first day after the murder in the park rousting drug houses. She could have seen her there. She looked like a user. The ivy vine tattoos on her arms did not hide her needle marks.

The woman from the park had had those same tattoos. And the same purple hair. Carson had made the notification to the woman's next of kin; did he recognize this woman? Was she related to the murder victim?

Juliette looked up to try to catch his attention, and the girl took that second to try to run. She leaped over the suitcase that Sasha had gotten the hit on and ran past the line for the bus.

"Gage!" Juliette yelled at her co-worker.

Without waiting to see if Carson followed, Juliette dropped Sasha's leash, knowing she'd stay with the suitcase, and started running after the girl. She couldn't let her get away. This woman—who looked so much like the murder victim—might be the best clue to finding the killer.

*This was not good.*

The bitch should have left town days ago—right after her sister's death—if she'd wanted to live. Hadn't her sister's murder been a lesson to her?

*Don't cross your bosses...*

Sure, he'd been told to leave town and he hadn't yet. But they didn't understand he had unfinished business. He was not about to leave witnesses alive.

And apparently, they'd been relieved, too, that he hadn't left when they'd realized the dead woman had not acted alone. They wanted their loose ends cleaned up, so maybe they would understand that he had to clean up his, as well.

They also wanted to send a message to their other associates: *You stole product from them and tried to sell it to someone else, and you were going to wind up dead.*

He stared through the scope of his long gun as he moved the barrel around—trying to find her.

Her purple hair made it easy enough to pick her out of the crowd. That and the fact that she was running.

He groaned. He wasn't the only one who'd made her. Those damn Red Ridge cops were getting in the way again. Then he saw the blond hair of the female officer who pursued her.

And he grinned with happiness. Maybe his luck had begun to change.

He was about to hit two birds with one stone…

After waking up alone in her house, Blake had called the bodyguards on her protection duty. They had assured him that they were close to Juliette, and that they wouldn't let anything happen to her.

But Blake had been compelled to join them again.

It wasn't just that he'd lost a little faith in them after the night before. It was also that he had an odd feeling he might not see Juliette again. So he was driving to the bus terminal where the bodyguards had told him they'd followed her from the police department.

Why did Finn keep sending her out in the field?

While he might not have been able to force her to stay in the safe house, he could have assigned her desk duty. Or suspended her completely until the killer was caught.

The man had not let up any on his attempts on her life. In fact, he'd seemed to get bolder. That attempt last night…

Blake shuddered as he remembered rushing into the stairwell to find the man's hands locked around Juliette's throat. She was strong. But the man had been stronger. If Blake hadn't shown up, he would have killed her for certain.

It was too dangerous for her to be anywhere but that safe house with their daughter.

That was where she needed to be—with Pandora.

A twinge struck his heart when he remembered that the little girl was why Juliette had come to see him at the hotel the night before.

Because he'd disappointed their daughter…

Already.

Evidently, he was his father's son. He remembered all the times he'd waited by the door for Fenwick to pick him for some promised outing. Only to have his father never show up…

All the times he'd searched the stands during football, basketball or baseball games to see if his father had come to watch, like he'd promised. But even on those rare instances when Fenwick had shown, he'd been on the phone with someone—too preoccupied with business or women to actually watch Blake play.

That long-ago disappointment in his father turned into

disappointment in himself now. Had he made Pandora feel like that—the way his father had made him feel?

He was also frustrated because he didn't know what to do. Did he get closer to the child and risk disappointing her even more than he already had?

Or did he figure out how to be a better father than Fenwick Colton had been to him and his sisters?

Maybe Juliette could teach him how. For the little girl's entire life, Juliette had been her father as well as her mother. She'd been everything to Pandora.

So why wasn't she with the child now? Why did she keep putting herself at risk to catch this killer?

He sighed again—because he knew. She needed to make sure the little girl was safe, and the only way to do that was to catch and put away the killer who'd threatened her.

He pulled his rental vehicle into the parking lot of the bus terminal and looked around for the bodyguards. As usual, he couldn't see their SUV; Finn had said he would only allow them to follow Juliette if they stayed out of the way of his officers. Blake saw two Red Ridge K9 unit patrol cars.

Juliette was not here alone.

He should have felt better, but he still had a heavy pressure in his chest. Maybe that was just his disappointment over how his parenting had started off.

Or maybe it was still that fear that he might not see Juliette again.

But then he did—as she ran through the parking lot—chasing some girl with purple hair and torn jeans.

Instinctively he reached for the door handle to push it open and step out.

The woman was obviously not the killer. So Juliette was chasing her for another reason. And he shouldn't intervene in police department work. He might jeopardize the arrest.

And infuriate Juliette even more than his presence usually did. But he couldn't stay in the car and just watch, either. He pushed open the door and stepped onto the parking lot. Heat radiated up from the asphalt.

The temperature didn't seem to bother the two women—who ran flat-out across the lot—in his direction. The purple-haired girl seemed desperate to escape the officer. But Juliette was determined, too, and closing the distance between them. Just as Juliette leaped toward the runner, shots rang out. Both women fell to the hot asphalt.

Had Juliette knocked them to the ground?

Or had a bullet?

# *Chapter 15*

Blood spatters dripped down Juliette's face. She wiped them away with a trembling hand. What the hell had just happened? She'd heard the gun shots—just as she had already been falling, knocking the woman to the ground.

She hadn't acted fast enough, though. She hadn't been able to draw her weapon from her holster to return fire. But she hadn't needed to. The bodyguards had jumped out of wherever they'd been hiding to return fire. They'd undoubtedly saved her life, just as they had the night before.

Once again, the killer had chosen a higher vantage point, like the roof of the greenhouse at the plant nursery from where he'd shot at her and had hit Dean instead.

Blake was standing over her now, staring down at

her. "Are you okay?" he asked, his voice gruff. His gaze appeared focused on her face and the blood droplets she'd smeared across it.

She nodded and tried to see where the killer might have shot from. He must have been on the roof of the hotel near the bus terminal. The bodyguards had gone after him. But she suspected that just like last night, the killer would have already escaped.

He moved so quickly. His wounded shoulder—which she'd shot in the park—must not have bothered him at all. She wished she'd shot him somewhere else that day—that she'd been able to stop him from hurting anyone else.

Like Dean…

And Blake…

And this poor girl…

"But there's blood…" Blake murmured.

"It's not mine." She glanced down at the prone body of the girl she'd been chasing. There was no need to check for a pulse. The girl had been struck in the head. She hadn't had a chance.

But had she been the intended target? Or like Dean Landon, had she taken a bullet meant for Juliette?

*I'm sorry*…she silently told her.

Juliette had only meant to arrest her. Not for her to die…

"Are you okay?" Carson Gage asked as he and the German shepherd joined her. Sasha was also with him, following the suitcase he carried. The girl's suitcase.

She would not be needing it anymore.

Juliette nodded. "I'm fine. You should take Justice and see if you can track the killer."

Carson nodded, but he didn't rush off. He must have thought the same thing she did—that it was too late. The killer was long gone again. "I called it in," he said. "But it doesn't look like an ambulance is going to be necessary."

"No." Instead of leaving in the back seat of a police car, the girl would be leaving in a body bag.

"This suitcase was hers, I'm assuming," Carson remarked. His eyes narrowed as he stared down at the body, focusing on the woman's face. "She looks familiar…"

"She looks like the woman from the park," Juliette said.

And Carson nodded. "I think it's her sister. I didn't get a good look at her when I notified the parents about the first victim. She wouldn't come out onto the porch where I was talking to them."

Like maybe she hadn't wanted him to get a good look at her. Or maybe she hadn't been curious about what had happened to her sister because she'd already known. Maybe she'd even known her sister's killer…

*Damn it!*

A potential real lead to the killer was gone. So maybe the woman hadn't just been in the wrong place at the wrong time. Maybe the bullet she'd taken had actually been meant for her and not for Juliette instead.

But still she felt a twinge of guilt along with her disappointment in losing the lead.

She had a feeling the girl would have been alive if

Juliette hadn't been the one who'd discovered her standing with that suitcase in line for the bus.

Blake had witnessed a murder himself now, so maybe he could relate to Pandora—if she brought up what she'd seen that day in the park. As he did for business meetings, he had prepared himself for every possible scenario that might happen during his visit with his daughter.

He'd had time to think about it while the bodyguards had smuggled him into the safe house. But now, standing in the doorway of the bedroom in which she was staying, he could only stare at her.

She played with some dolls. A trio of them sat in miniature chairs around a miniature table in the corner of the room. Pandora poured them each imaginary tea from a small plastic teapot.

Before he could think of anything to say, she glanced up and noticed him in the doorway. "Daddy!" she exclaimed. She leaped from her chair and rushed toward him.

And his heart stopped. Nobody had ever been as happy to see him as she was. And she didn't even know him…

But maybe that was why she was so happy.

She held up her arms, and for a second Blake froze, uncertain what she wanted. He had never been around little kids before. Then, just as disappointment was beginning to flash across her face, he lifted her in his arms and drew her close to his chest.

She threw her arms around his neck and pressed her

cheek to his. And his heart lurched with the overwhelming force of the love rushing through him. He'd never felt anything like this before.

She leaned back and stared at his face, as if trying to memorize it. Maybe that was because she'd seen it only once and then he hadn't come around again.

He'd been such a fool. And a coward...

Sure, she was in danger. But the bodyguards took extra precautions to make sure there was no way anyone would realize they were heading to the safe house. They never drove their SUVs—always some other kind of vehicle they found, like that van from the hospital or utility trucks.

Right now, the killer, if he was for any reason following Blake, would think he was back in his hotel suite. But Blake suspected the killer was instead parked somewhere outside the Red Ridge Police Department, which was where Juliette had been heading after leaving the crime scene at the bus terminal.

She had to be safe at the police department. But Blake had a team of bodyguards stationed outside it, as well. He'd brought in more guards from the security agency to make sure there were enough to keep her and Pandora safe.

"I'm so glad you're here," the little girl told him. "You're just in time for the party." She wriggled down from his arms but grabbed his hand with her tiny one and tugged him toward the table of dolls.

He had sisters, so he was not unfamiliar with tea parties. But it had been a long while since he'd been forced to participate in one. Pandora had a sweeter way of manipulating him than his sisters had had, though. There was no one holding his matchbox cars hostage until he drank several cups of fake tea.

He was here willingly. "I'm glad I didn't miss it," he told her.

She reached for one of the dolls to move it from the chair, but he knelt next to the table instead. "I can't take a seat from a lady," he told her.

"Why not?" she asked.

Of course her mother, who was tough and independent, would be teaching her daughter to be a little feminist, as well.

"It's just not the gentlemanly thing to do," he explained. "A gentleman always gives his seat to a lady."

Her little brow furrowed with confusion. Then she nodded. "And princes are gentlemen, right?"

Not some of the ones he'd met—the ones who were real royalty. Blake was just Red Ridge royalty—according to Juliette. And right now, with his cousin suspected of murder bringing to attention the horrendous crimes some of his other family members had committed, there was nothing advantageous to being a Colton.

Maybe that was why Juliette had never told him about his daughter. She hadn't wanted Pandora to be acknowledged as a Colton. At the moment, he couldn't blame her.

"Daddy?" she prodded him.

And he realized he hadn't answered her question. Because he wanted to be honest but appropriate with her, he replied, "All princes should be gentlemen."

She smiled and nodded in agreement. Then she handed him a cup of tea.

He passed the little plastic cup from hand to hand. "Ow, ow, that's hot!"

She giggled and acted as if her cup was too hot, as well. Then they kept playing like that—following each other's lead until they both collapsed into fits of laughter.

Blake had never felt the way he did with his daughter. Had never felt so much love...

Then he looked up and noticed that they were no longer alone. Someone leaned against the doorjamb, watching them. It wasn't the female cop, Elle Gage, who must have been assigned to protect Pandora 24-7. After letting him into the house, Elle had left him alone with his daughter.

The woman standing in the doorway was Juliette.

Her lashes fluttered as she blinked rapidly, as if fighting back the tears that glistened in her eyes. Then Pandora noticed her, too, and jumped up to throw herself into her mother's arms.

Juliette did not hesitate for even a fraction of a second. She clutched the little girl close and spun her around like they'd been separated for weeks instead of hours.

"Mommy, Mommy!" Pandora said. "You're just in time for our tea party! The tea's still hot."

"I see that," Juliette murmured. She must have been watching them for a while.

But Blake had been so enthralled with his daughter, he hadn't noticed Juliette's arrival. He noticed her now, though. She looked so beautiful, her hair down and loose around her bare shoulders. She wore another sleeveless blouse with a short skirt. This one was an off-white color that complemented her orange blouse.

Unlike him, Juliette settled onto one of the chairs—with the doll she'd displaced in her lap. The chair didn't break beneath her weight like it would have Blake's, but then, Juliette was so petite and light that he'd easily lifted her.

Pandora looked around the table, and a big smile spread across her face, making the dimple in her left cheek deepen. "The whole family's here now."

Blake felt another twinge in his heart, but he wasn't sure if it was love this time.

Or pure panic.


"She's supposedly my family!" Fenwick Colton bellowed. "I should damn well be allowed to see her."

Finn was the police chief. Not a family counselor. "I'm not getting involved in this," he told the man.

Fenwick was so fired up that instead of summoning Finn, he'd come down to the police department himself. He must have either bullied or charmed his way past Lorelei back to Finn's office.

Fortunately Juliette had already left for the day, or the older man might have demanded to see her, as well. Right now he was just focused on her daughter, though.

"You have her stashed away in some safe house," Fenwick said. "So you are involved."

"I'm protecting a witness to a murder," he said. And he was damn glad that he had. With all the attempts made on her mother's life, there was no way the child would have been safe if she hadn't been hidden away from the killer.

"She's a little girl," Fenwick said, and for once there seemed to be almost genuine empathy in his voice. But then he cleared his throat and mused, "It's just not for certain that she's Blake's little girl."

And the empathy was gone.

Finn swallowed a sigh of frustration as his head began to pound. Was he really related to this man? At least he wasn't his son—like poor Blake was.

"What do you know about her mother?" the mayor asked.

"That she's a damn fine officer," Finn said. "One of my finest."

"How *fine* is she?" The older man's eyes narrowed with suspicion. "Have you been involved with her, too?"

"Absolutely not." That was a line Finn would have never crossed—with any of his officers.

"What about anyone else? Has she ever been married or engaged?" Fenwick fired the questions at him. "Has she ever dated anybody else around here?"

Finn wasn't about to discuss Juliette Walsh's personal life—not that he thought she'd ever had much of one besides her daughter. Her life revolved around that little girl.

That was probably why she was so determined to catch the man who'd threatened the child. Even if her efforts cost her own life.

"I don't get involved with my officers," Finn said.

"And I don't get involved in their personal lives, either. You need to talk to your son about this."

Fenwick didn't bother swallowing his sigh; he expelled a long and ragged one. "Blake and I don't talk. We argue."

No wonder Blake had stayed away from Red Ridge for so many years. Finn didn't know what to say, so he remained silent. Maybe the mayor would get the hint that he was not going to participate in this conversation and leave.

"And why is Blake following this police officer around?" Fenwick asked. "He's not a cop or a bodyguard."

Finn shrugged. He'd already pointed that out to Blake to no avail. Maybe that was why father and son argued so much; they were too much alike. Stubborn and headstrong.

"She must mean something to him," Fenwick said, and now there was fear in his voice. "Maybe too much…"

Finn suspected the same. If a man was willing to put his life at risk for a woman, he must care about her.

"You don't think he'd do something crazy like propose to her, do you?" Fenwick asked, his voice cracking with very real fear and horror.

Finn shrugged again. "Like I said, Blake's the one you need to have this conversation with."

The older man shook his head. "No, you're the one who needs to catch Demi Colton and stop these killings of innocent men about to be married."

And now Finn understood why Fenwick was here. He

was worried that his son might become the next victim of the Groom Killer.

"I don't think you have to worry about Blake becoming a target," he said.

Juliette wasn't happy to have Blake following her around. And she had never told him about his child until he returned to Red Ridge.

No. Fenwick didn't need to worry about the Groom Killer going after his son; he needed to worry about the killer that was after Pandora and Juliette taking out Blake, too.

## Chapter 16

Standing in that doorway, watching Blake play and laugh with their daughter, had caused Juliette physical pain. She'd felt the pressure of guilt weighing so heavily on her that her heart ached with it. She never should have kept his daughter from him.

She should have told him. He'd had a right to know. And then, if he hadn't wanted to be involved in Pandora's life, it would have been his choice.

She never should have made that choice for him. Or for Pandora...

But along with the guilt, Juliette had felt another kind of pain as her heart had swelled with so much love she'd thought it might burst.

Pandora was so funny and sweet and smart. She was

an amazing little girl. And Juliette was so lucky she was hers. She had to make certain nothing happened to her.

But she didn't want anything to happen to Blake, either. He could have died the night before—when the gunman had fired all those shots in the stairwell.

"What's wrong, Mommy?" Pandora asked.

The tea party had ended a while ago, and the little girl was lying in bed now, her head on her pillow. Juliette knelt on one side of her twin bed, and Blake knelt on the other. Sasha had jumped onto the foot of the bed, spinning in circles like a cat until she settled onto the little girl's feet.

Sasha was missing Pandora nearly as much as Juliette was. That was why the beagle hadn't budged from the little girl's empty bed last night when Blake had arrived. She wondered how she would get her canine partner to leave her daughter tonight. She would have left the dog here—if she didn't need Sasha so much herself.

Pandora reached out and touched Juliette's forehead. "You have worry lines," she murmured.

And Juliette smiled with that love bursting inside her. Her little girl was so precocious.

Pandora turned to Blake. She reached out and touched the cut on his cheek. "Daddy has a line, too."

"It's just a scratch," he assured her. "No worry line."

But Juliette's were. She was worried that he could have been hurt so much worse than the concrete chips he must have had flushed out before he'd come to see her the night before.

Pandora smiled. "You are still handsome," she assured him. "Don't you think so, Mommy? Don't you think Daddy is a handsome prince?"

The little girl knew that Juliette did because she'd told her so in the stories she'd shared about her father. The imp was playing matchmaker.

And now panic struck Juliette's heart. Pandora had already called them a family during her tea party.

Was she setting her heart on them all being together?

Juliette smiled back at her daughter. But as a mother, she had to caution her. "Remember that Daddy doesn't live with us," she told her. "Daddy doesn't even live in Red Ridge."

Blake sucked in a breath. Then he forced a smile and remarked, "Would I be better-looking if I did?"

He would be—then Juliette wouldn't be so worried about him breaking her and Pandora's hearts.

"I just want to remind Pandora that we can't have family tea parties every day. Eventually you'll be going back to your home."

"Where do you live, Daddy?" the little girl asked. "In a castle?"

"Right now I live in a hotel suite," he said.

And Juliette wondered about his home in other countries. Did he just live out of hotel suites in them, too?

That was no kind of life for a child. But then, because of her, he hadn't known he had a child.

"What's a hotel sweet?" asked the little girl. "Is it made of candy?"

He chuckled and leaned forward to press his lips against her forehead. "No. Then little girls like you would eat it all up."

She smiled. "Yes, I would."

How had he gotten to know their daughter so quickly? How had they bonded already? Was it because they had always had a bond but never known about it—because of her?

The guilt pulled heavily on Juliette again. But she pushed it aside to focus on what was best for Pandora. And she—and the life they'd built in Red Ridge—was.

"I love our house," Pandora told her father. "I love my room. And my toys. And Mommy tucking me in with Sasha sleeping on my bed."

Sasha was on the bed now. That was why she and Blake had had to kneel on the floor. While neither the beagle nor the little girl was that big, combined they took up the entire twin.

"When can we go home, Mommy?" she asked. And finally her eyelids began to droop as she struggled to stay awake. No doubt the little smarty had figured out that once she fell asleep, Juliette left.

"As soon as we put the bad man in jail, we'll go home," Juliette assured her.

Despite the blankets and the dog covering her, the little girl shivered.

And Juliette regretted bringing up the bad man. Pandora didn't have imaginary monsters to fear; she had a real one.

"It'll be soon," Juliette promised. She would make sure she wasn't lying. She would keep that promise to her daughter. She had to—for all their sakes.

As if taking her at her word, Pandora slipped into slumber. A breath sighed out between her lips.

Juliette kissed her forehead and rose from the floor. Blake stood up, too, and reached for her across the bed. But Juliette pulled away and walked into the hall.

"You don't have to be the one to get him," Blake said. "You can let someone else catch him."

"Like they caught the Groom Killer?" She shook her head. "We're already spread too thin. I need to stay on the job. I need to stay focused."

So she couldn't get involved any deeper with him. He was messing with her sleep and her head and her heart.

Blake gestured toward the bedroom door she'd pulled mostly closed. "She's the one you need to focus on," he said.

She sucked in a breath. "How dare you critique my parenting! I've been doing it alone just fine all these years."

"That was your choice," he said. "Not mine."

"What is your choice?" she asked. "Are you going to stick around and be a real parent? Or will you be taking off once she's no longer in danger?"

He sucked in a breath now. But he just shook his head. "We can't talk about that here."

He was right. She didn't want Pandora or Elle to overhear their argument. And she knew they were going to argue. But that was all they were going to do.

She couldn't make love with him again—because she was starting to fall in love with him. And she wasn't about to risk her heart on a man who was leaving—again.

The bodyguards smuggled out Juliette and Blake as carefully as they'd smuggled them into the safe house.

Blake wasn't worried that anyone would find the place where Finn had stashed their daughter. That was why he wished Juliette would stay there.

Instead she'd insisted on coming back to her little house on that suburban street in Red Ridge. He was worried that the killer would find her here—easily.

She was making it even easier for him when she sat down on her front steps instead of unlocking the door to go inside. The beagle, off her leash, meandered around the small front yard, sniffing the grass.

"You should come back to my hotel suite," he said.

"Because it's so safe there?" she asked with a disparaging roll of her beautiful blue eyes.

"It will be now," he promised. He'd brought in more bodyguards from the protection agency. "The hotel stepped up security."

She pointed at Sasha and in a snobbish-sounding voice remarked, "The Colton Plaza Hotel does not allow animals in their rooms."

Blake chuckled at her tone. "They make exceptions for service dogs and that's what Sasha is. She does an incredible service by getting drugs off the street."

Juliette sighed. "That wasn't all we got off the streets today."

"The girl…" Blake said. She'd looked so young. He'd overheard Juliette and the detective talking about her being the sister of the murder victim from the park. "Why do you think he wanted them both dead?"

She shook her head. "I think someone else wanted them dead. Whoever she'd taken that suitcase of drugs from, just like her sister had. The man was just carrying out the order…"

"A hired assassin? That's what this guy is who's after you and Pandora?" He shuddered. But of course, it all made sense. That was why he was so good that last night he'd slipped past even the renowned security agency Blake had hired.

Maybe he was too good…

"You're not safe here," he persisted. "You and Sasha need to come back to the hotel with me."

"No," she said. "I need to sleep tonight."

"You'll sleep better when you know you're safe," he insisted. And so would he.

She shook her head again. "You and I both know we won't sleep if I go back to your suite."

His body tensed thinking about it—about being inside her again. He fit so perfectly, as if they'd been made for each other.

"And that's a problem?"

Now she nodded. "Yes. It's bad enough that I'm worried you're going to break my daughter's—"

"*Our* daughter's," he interrupted her as a fierce possessiveness overcame him.

"Pandora," she said instead. "I think you're going to break her heart. I don't want you breaking mine, too."

Frustration nagged at him. "I don't understand you. Last night you were mad at me for not going to see Pandora. And now you're mad that I did."

She uttered a weary sigh. "I just don't want her getting hurt."

"Neither do I." But he was very afraid that he

might—inadvertently—hurt her just because he had no damn idea how to be a father.

"If you're going to leave soon and not come back very often, it might be best if you don't see her now," Juliette said. "If you just let her go…"

The thought gripped his heart in a tight vise, painfully squeezing. He shook his head. "No."

Now that he knew he had a daughter, he couldn't just walk away. He could never return to the life he'd had before he'd learned the truth. So what the hell was he going to do? Not about just Pandora but also about his business?

He needed time to think, and that was impossible to do around Juliette. She was too beautiful, too sexy, too damn distracting…

She was smart not to come back to his hotel suite. But he didn't think she should stay here, either.

She stared up at him through eyes that were heavy with exhaustion. "Please," she implored him. "Think about what's best for her."

"I don't have to think about that," Blake said. "You are. She can't lose her mother, so you need to stop putting yourself in danger."

He grimaced as he remembered watching her fall in the parking lot today and then running up to see that blood spattered across her face. For a long, horrifying moment, he'd thought she'd been hit. Then she'd moved, and relief had rushed through him.

"I have the training and experience to handle the dangers of my job," she said. "You don't. You have no business following me around all day."

"You don't want Pandora to get hurt," he said. "Neither do I. You getting hurt will hurt her." Far worse than if he left Red Ridge.

"It would hurt her to lose you, too," Juliette said. "And that's more likely to happen if you insist on sticking so close to me. You saw what happened to that girl today."

He flinched. "Yes, but that was because of the drugs she was carrying."

"We don't know that for certain," Juliette said. "The bullet could have been meant for me—not her."

True. And that was what he'd thought when it had happened. "You need to go into that safe house with Pandora," he said.

"What I need to do is sleep," she said. And she rose from the porch steps.

He couldn't argue with her. Being exhausted was not going to help her find the gunman—or survive his next attempt on her life.

And Blake knew there would be another attempt. This assassin was obviously determined to get rid of her.

He glanced around, but it was so dark beyond the circle of light from the streetlamp in front of her house. While there was no patrol car yet, the bodyguards were out there—somewhere. They would make certain nothing happened to her.

He hesitated before turning away from her, though. Maybe it was because he wanted to kiss her good-night. But this wasn't a date. And he knew if he kissed her, that the night would not be over—or at least, he wouldn't want it to be over. He would want to make love to her again and again like he had the night before and that night five years ago when Pandora had been conceived.

"Sasha," Juliette called to the beagle. The dog immediately headed up the porch steps with her.

She had the bodyguards and her canine partner. She didn't need Blake.

But he was beginning to feel as if he needed her.

"Good night, Blake," she said.

She was dismissing him. He knew that. But he wondered if it was just for the night or for always. She'd made it clear that she didn't want him following her anymore, and he didn't think it was just because that girl had died today.

She was determined to protect her life herself. Now she was also determined to protect her heart. From him...

"Good night," he murmured back, but she was already unlocking her door to step inside the house. The dog rushed through before Juliette could enter. She followed Sasha inside and closed the door without so much as a glance back in Blake's direction.

He stayed on the front walk for another long moment, staring up at the house. So he noticed the flash even before he heard the shot.

Someone had fired a gun inside the house.

# Chapter 17

The way Sasha had hurried inside the house had fore-warned Juliette that it was not empty. That was why she hadn't looked back at Blake. She hadn't wanted him to interfere and get caught in the middle as she drew her weapon and returned the fire of whomever had started shooting the minute she'd closed her door.

Glass shattered behind her as bullets struck the picture window. She hoped Blake was no longer standing out there, that he'd turned and walked away. Far away…

"Put down your weapon!" she shouted—even though she couldn't see the intruder. "You're under arrest!"

A chuckle rang out of the darkness. And she fired in its direction. Glass broke. She hadn't shot in the direction of a window, so it must have been a picture frame or a mirror. She hoped the former. The last thing she needed was any more bad luck.

"Put down your weapon!" she shouted again.

There was no chuckle this time. No response at all. Had she hit him?

Sasha's barking, which had been incessant since she'd pushed ahead of Juliette through the door, finally stopped. Had the beagle been hit?

Juliette could see nothing in the darkness. But before she could fumble around for a light switch or a lamp, she heard a noise behind her.

Had he circled around her?

Her finger twitched on the trigger as she prepared to pull and fire again. But then a deep voice called out, "Juliette! Are you okay?"

And she cursed and lowered the barrel.

But more shots rang out.

She fell from the heavy weight on top of her as she lay back on the hardwood floor. But the shots weren't close. Someone was firing outside her house. Blake was the one who'd knocked her to the ground.

The killer and the bodyguards must have been exchanging gunfire. And she could hear Sasha barking, too.

"Are you all right?" Blake asked.

"No, thanks to you," she murmured as she struggled to get up. She needed to get outside—to handle Sasha and to find the killer.

And maybe that was why Blake remained on top of her, his hard body heavy on hers—because he didn't want her confronting the killer again.

She shoved his shoulders, trying to push him back. "Get off me! I need to get out there!"

"You need to stay here," Blake said.

The gunfire had stopped. But she heard sirens now, wailing in the distance. And she felt like wailing in frustration. He'd been right here.

So close…

And yet he'd escaped her once again. She had no doubt that he had escaped the bodyguards, too—because she could hear Sasha's barking grow fainter and fainter. She was still pursuing the intruder.

She shoved harder. "Blake, let me up. I need to back up Sasha." So many canines were injured or killed just doing their jobs—because they wouldn't stop until their handlers told them to.

Sasha wasn't as big as some of the other breeds in the K9 unit, but she was every bit as fearless.

Finally Blake budged, and Juliette squirmed out from beneath him. Then she rushed out the back door. The killer must have left it open when he'd run out.

"Sasha!" she called out, her heart pounding with fear for her partner. "Sasha! Heel!"

She could hear the dog whimpering somewhere in the dark. Had she been hurt?

She started across the backyard, but she wasn't alone. Blake had followed her from the house, and he kept reaching for her arm, trying to pull her back.

"Juliette, it isn't safe."

"He's gone," one of the bodyguards remarked as the burly man rushed up to join them. "He fired off a couple of rounds as he came out of the house, but he kept running."

So Juliette had not hit him inside the house. He wasn't injured other than his previous shoulder wound. And that hadn't slowed him down at all yet.

The guy just kept coming.

She sighed with frustration and tugged away from Blake's hand on her arm. "I need to find Sasha." She met the beagle halfway across the backyard. The dog whimpered when Juliette touched her side. Had she been shot?

"I need to get her to the vet!" Juliette said as concern gripped her. "She's hurt."

Before she could lift the animal, Blake was there, gently picking up the dog.

"Be careful with her," Juliette implored him as she blinked against the tears stinging her eyes. "Please, be careful!"

"I will," he said.

And he was, because the dog didn't whimper again even as he loaded her into Juliette's car. They were just backing out of the driveway when the first patrol car arrived. Where had it been?

Had there been another murder tonight? Was that why her coworkers hadn't been watching her? Of course, the bodyguards were the ones who'd been getting her in and out of the safe house, and they did their job so well that they must have lost the patrol car, too.

Maybe her coworkers had thought she would return to the Colton Plaza Hotel after seeing Pandora.

"Sasha's hurt," she told the dark-haired officer when

Dante Mancuso rushed up to her car. "We need to get her to the vet."

"Go! Go," he urged her.

"The bodyguards can tell you what happened," she said as she eased her foot off the brake and started backing into the street.

Mancuso murmured something as she drove away. Something that sounded like, "I can guess..."

Everybody could—because it seemed as though anyone close to Juliette got hurt. She glanced across the console at Blake. He'd nearly been shot the night before. It was only a matter of time before he got hurt again.

Or worse...

Patience Colton had no life. At least no social life. Her life was her job, and the top priority of her job was to take care of Red Ridge's canine force. She rushed around her office, making sure she had everything ready.

She hoped it wasn't a bullet that had injured the dog. If it was, she would be prepared. But she wasn't prepared to turn around and see her brother carrying in the wounded beagle. She stared, stunned, at his sudden appearance. "Blake, what the hell..."

"Where do you want her, Patience?" he asked.

She gestured to the stainless-steel examination table. "There. What happened?" And what did her brother have to do with it?

A blond-haired woman followed him into the office. It took Patience a few seconds to recognize her without her uniform. But then she glanced at the dog again. "Sasha..." And Juliette Walsh was her handler.

"What happened?" she asked the female officer.

"I don't know," Juliette replied. "She went after a perp. I don't think he shot her because I don't see an entrance wound."

Patience turned her attention to the dog. She would deal with her brother later. "No blood…"

Juliette's breath shuddered out. But a lack of blood wasn't always a good thing. There might have been no blood because the injuries and bleeding were all internal.

Patience ran her hands along the dog's side, and Sasha whimpered softly and arched her neck. Patience rubbed the dog's head between her ears. "It's okay…" she soothed her. To Juliette, she said, "I'm going to take some X-rays. You two should step outside."

Juliette hesitated, clearly unwilling to leave her partner alone. But Blake slid his arm around the slight woman and escorted her toward the waiting room.

And Patience drew in a deep breath. She wasn't just worried about the dog. Now she was worried about her brother, too. She had never seen him look at anyone the way he'd looked at Juliette—with such caring and concern.

Had her father been right? Should she not have called Blake to come back to Red Ridge? Because if he had fallen for the beautiful K9 cop, he would be putting his life in danger—from the Groom Killer.

But that wasn't all the danger he faced if he was involved with Juliette Walsh. She'd heard about the murder in the park—the one Juliette's daughter had witnessed.

She tensed as she suddenly understood the message her father had left her. The voice mail had told her that she needed to talk some sense into her brother. She hadn't had a chance or the inclination to call him back yet.

But now she knew what he was talking about...

Juliette Walsh.

She pushed concern for her brother aside, though, as she focused on the beagle instead. Once she read the X-rays she'd taken, she finally blew out the breath she'd been holding. She opened the door to her exam room and gestured for Blake and Juliette to step back inside.

"How bad is it?" Juliette asked, her blue eyes glistening with unshed tears. She really loved her partner.

How did she feel about Patience's brother?

Patience smiled reassuringly. "She's fine. Just bruised. I would say someone kicked her side."

Juliette leaned over her dog and pressed her head against the dog's as she rubbed her neck. "You are such a good girl. You tried to get him..."

"Do you think she got a piece of him?" Blake asked.

Juliette stepped back, and Patience looked in the dog's mouth. A few strands of denim were stuck between her teeth. "Looks like she might have gotten his jeans."

"Good dog," Blake praised the canine, too.

"What's going on?" Patience asked. And she wasn't asking about just what had happened to Sasha. She suspected it was that other killer on the loose who'd kicked her. She was asking what was going on with them. How did Blake even know Juliette Walsh?

"The man who killed the woman in the park was in my house," Juliette told her.

And apparently so was Blake.

"Sasha alerted me to his presence," Juliette said as she lovingly ran her hand over the dog's head again. "If she hadn't, I might not have survived."

The color drained from Blake's face, leaving him looking pale and shaken. The thought of losing Juliette obviously upset him. What did she mean to him?

"Are you okay?" Patience asked her. She narrowed her eyes and studied the woman. She looked as upset as Blake was. She truly had had a close call.

Juliette nodded. "Yes, I'm fine—as long as she will be…" She stared down at her dog.

Patience smiled. She loved how close every K9 officer was to his or her canine partner. But then, that was bound to happen when they trusted each other with their lives. Patience's smile slid into a frown. "I heard you're in danger. And your daughter, too." She glanced at her brother. "I'm sorry…"

"We'll catch him," Juliette said, but she still sounded scared and uncertain.

"We will," Blake insisted.

"We?" Patience asked, and her control on her curiosity snapped. "What the hell are you talking about? You're a businessman, not a police officer!" She hadn't called him to Red Ridge to lose him.

"That's what I keep telling him," Juliette said. "He needs to stop trying to protect me."

Blake shook his head. "I can't."

"Why not?" Patience asked. Was he in love with the beautiful K9 cop?

"Because she's the mother of my daughter."

Patience's knees shook for a moment, and she nearly dropped. But she clutched the edge of the exam table and stayed upright. Sasha licked her hand, as if in commiseration or out of gratitude.

Her brother was a father? She was an aunt?

"No way," she murmured.

And she couldn't help but think that her dad was finally right about something. She never should have called Blake back to Red Ridge—because it was clear to her now that he was in danger.

Blake waited for Juliette to step across the threshold and enter his suite. She hesitated so long that he was tempted to pick her up like he had that night so long ago and carry her across it.

But he'd freaked himself out when he'd done that because it had felt too much like a honeymoon. And he'd never intended to get married. Then.

That hadn't changed, even though he knew he had a daughter now. Sure, he'd never intended to be a father, either, but that choice had been taken from him.

And he wasn't mad about that at all.

Juliette seemed mad, though. But then, she hadn't wanted to come back here when he'd asked her earlier. It had taken her house getting shot up and her canine partner hurt for her to agree to return to the suite with him.

"You hadn't told her," she murmured as she finally stepped inside with him.

Before he closed the door, he glanced into the hallway and expelled a breath of relief to see one of the bodyguards standing sentry. They would be safe tonight.

"What?" he asked, his brow furrowed. He couldn't figure out why she was angry.

"You hadn't told your sister about Pandora," she said.

He shrugged. "I'm not that close to my family. You realize that…" She knew more about him than anyone else—especially his family.

"Is that the real reason you didn't tell her?" she asked.

He nodded. "What other reason could I have?"

"You're ashamed of her. Of us…"

Now he understood why she was angry. But her accusation made him angry, too. "Stop calling me a snob," he said. "I don't care that you used to be a maid. I respect that you have always been a hard worker. And there is no way I would ever be ashamed of Pandora." His voice cracked with emotion when he added, "She's amazing…"

And not just because she was his. He would have thought she was special even if he wasn't related to her.

"Yes, she is," Juliette agreed. And there was so much pride and love in her voice.

"My father knows," he admitted. "I thought that he'd probably told my sisters." He was surprised that he hadn't, but then, his father wasn't convinced that the little girl was Blake's. He wanted to see her first.

And even then, he probably still wouldn't believe it.

He stepped closer to Juliette and tipped up her chin

so that he could stare deeply into her beautiful eyes. "You have to stop this…thinking I would be ashamed of you," he said. "You and Pandora should be ashamed of me."

Her lips curved into a smile. "Really?"

"Yes," he said. "I'm a Colton."

She tilted her head.

"Being a Colton isn't always exactly a source of pride," he told her. "My cousin's wanted for murder."

"It's looking less and less like Demi is the Groom Killer," Juliette said.

He shrugged. "It doesn't matter. Other members of distant branches of the Colton family have been killers."

"So what are you telling me?" she asked. "That I should sleep with one eye open?"

"Maybe you shouldn't sleep at all," he told her.

She narrowed her eyes with suspicion, but she grinned. "You told me that I would be able to sleep here."

He had—when he'd finally convinced her to come back with him. Patience had had her leave Sasha with her for the night—just to make sure the beagle got a chance to rest and recover.

"Do you want to sleep?" he asked. She looked exhausted—with dark circles beneath her eyes. He really should let her sleep.

But she shook her head, stepped closer and pressed her lips to his. Against his mouth, she murmured, "I want you…"

He wanted her, too—so badly. But he was worried that she was totally exhausting herself trying to catch this killer, so he pulled back and stared down at her. "You should sleep. You need your rest."

"I need…"

He waited for her to say—to say that she needed him. But instead she said, "I need this…" She yanked up his shirt and pulled it over his head. "I have all this adrenaline…"

He could understand that—after the shooting. His pulse was racing, too, but it wasn't because of the bullets that had been flying. It was because of her.

She unbuttoned his jeans and jerked down the zipper. Then her fingers were closing around him, stroking him…

He groaned as his control snapped. Then he swung her up in his arms and carried her into the bedroom. Just as quickly as she'd undressed him, he undressed her until finally they were skin to skin.

Almost as close as they could be…

But he wanted to be closer. He grabbed a condom packet and tore it open. She pulled out the condom before he could and rolled it down his shaft.

He groaned again and pushed her back onto the bed. But he didn't immediately join their bodies. Instead he made sure she was ready for him—with his fingers, with his mouth…

She squirmed against the mattress and arched against him, crying out as he gave her pleasure. He wanted to give her more. But before he could, she was grabbing his shoulders and pulling him up the bed. Then she shoved him onto his back and straddled him.

Maybe—with all the attempts on her life—she

needed to feel in control again—because she controlled the pace, sliding up and down, rocking back and forth... driving him out of his mind.

Tension gripped his body, and sweat beaded on his brow and upper lip. Then she leaned down and kissed it away, kissing him deeply.

He slid his hands up from her hips to her breasts and teased her nipples into taut points with his fingers. Then he arched up from the bed and closed his mouth around one.

She cried out as she came, her inner muscles gripping and convulsing around his shaft. He thrust up, seeking his release, as he gripped her hips and moved her up and down, and finally the tension inside him broke.

A low, deep groan ripped from his throat as pleasure overwhelmed him.

She moved off him and dropped onto the bed, trying to catch her breath. He was panting, too. He forced himself up, though, and into the bathroom to clean up. When he returned to the bed, she was asleep—her breathing slow and even.

Careful not to disturb her, he slid into bed next to her and pulled up the sheets. She rolled over, and it was as if she'd been looking for him because she settled against him. Her head against his shoulder, her arm across his chest.

He settled his arm around her and held her closely. She was safe now. But he knew that once she awoke she would insist on leaving—on putting herself in danger again.

And he was afraid that it was only a matter of time

before one of the killer's attempts to get her proved successful. It was only a matter of time before Pandora lost her mother and Blake lost…

Everything.

That was what Juliette was beginning to mean to him: everything.

# Chapter 18

"Is she okay?" Juliette anxiously asked as Patience Colton brought Sasha out of the kennel the next morning.

The beagle wagged her tail and greeted Juliette, who had dropped to her knees, with wet kisses. Her entire brown-and-white body moved with excitement at seeing her. And not even a whimper slipped out.

"She's fine," Patience assured her. "I gave her a sedative to calm her down last night, so she would sleep. And she's raring to go this morning."

Juliette breathed a sigh of relief. "I'm so glad."

"Like I told you last night, she still needs to take it easy for a couple of days, though," Patience advised her. "Just until the swelling goes down."

"Will that be long enough?" Juliette asked. A couple of days wasn't too long—not after she'd worried that she'd lost her last night when she'd heard the whimpering in the dark.

"Yes," Patience said.

"Thank you," Juliette said. "I need her."

"What about my brother?" Patience asked.

Juliette glanced uneasily around the training center. The vet was not alone in the long brick building. Hayley Patton worked as a trainer there, but she must have been late because Juliette didn't see the blonde woman when she looked around. Of course she'd heard that Hayley was using her fiancé's death as her excuse for everything—for calling in sick to work, for being late... for not paying her bills.

"What do you mean?" Juliette asked Patience, even though she was pretty certain she knew. Blake's sister was asking her what her intentions were for her younger brother.

"Do you need him?" Patience asked.

Juliette was afraid that she did—especially after last night. She'd felt so safe and secure in his arms that she'd slept more deeply than she had in a long time. But she shouldn't have felt safe with him because she had a feeling that he could hurt her badly if she let herself fall for him.

"I don't need him," Juliette said. "I can take care of myself. I've been doing it for years."

"And your daughter," Patience added. "You've taken care of Pandora for years on your own, too. Why did you tell Blake now?"

"He saw her," Juliette admitted. "And he figured it out."

"And if he hadn't?" his sister asked.

Juliette tensed. She'd known he was back in town because everybody in Red Ridge had been talking about his return. She'd even known where to find him. But she hadn't sought him out—hadn't gone to tell him that he was a father despite Elle urging her to do it.

Patience waited and watched, then nodded. "If you really don't need my brother, then you should let him go now," she said.

"I don't have him," Juliette said. While she'd admitted to being afraid that he might break her heart along with Pandora's, he had expressed no such fear. His heart was safe from her. While he wanted her physically, he wasn't as emotionally invested as she was.

"It certainly looked like you had him last night," Patience said.

Juliette's face flushed with embarrassment. But the vet couldn't know what they'd done in Blake's suite. She must have been talking about the way Blake had acted when they were in her office.

"And he's been following you, trying to protect you," Patience said as she glanced around the kennels. "I'm surprised he's not here now."

Juliette had snuck out again before he'd awakened. But she wasn't about to share that with his sister. Her face heated even more with embarrassment, though.

And Patience nodded again, as if she'd figured it out anyway.

"I don't want Blake following me," Juliette said. Maybe his sister could talk some sense into him, but she didn't think it was likely since she and the chief had already failed. "I don't want him putting himself in danger."

"Then cut him loose," Patience said. "Before he gets hurt. Make it clear you want nothing to do with him. Or he might wind up the next victim of the Groom Killer."

Juliette gasped. "We're not getting married. I don't even think he's going to stay in Red Ridge." And if that was the case, she and Pandora were the ones who would wind up getting hurt. Not Blake.

But his sister was right—for all their sakes. She had to cut him loose.

*Damn it!*

She'd done it again. She'd slipped away while Blake had been sleeping. Fortunately the bodyguards had stayed on her. They'd assured him a patrol car had been following her, as well. So she was safe…

Was he?

After last night, he knew he was beginning to fall for her. He shouldn't. He still couldn't trust her. She hadn't told him about his daughter. Even now, she admonished him for not seeing Pandora enough while pushing him away when he had. Did she want him to be part of their lives?

Her indecisiveness left him wary—so wary that he was meeting with a lawyer who had called him at his father's urging, and Blake had agreed to talk with him.

"I want to make sure my daughter is taken care of," Blake said.

Unlike his father, Blake made that his first priority. He wanted to make sure Pandora always had what she

needed. That was why he wanted to keep Juliette safe—
because she needed her mother more than anything else.

He really should have skipped this meeting until
after the killer was caught. He couldn't really focus on
this—or the business he'd tried conducting earlier—
with thoughts of Juliette in his head. He remembered
that flash of gunfire behind her picture window before
the glass had exploded.

Her falling in the parking lot the day before…

Yes, it was only a matter of time before the killer
tried again. He had to be caught.

"You can draw up some trust papers for her," Blake
said, "and set up another meeting with me to sign those."
He also wanted to give Juliette a lump sum amount of
cash for back child support. She'd been caring for their
daughter alone for much too long.

The lawyer was obviously a friend of his father's because he looked at Blake the same way his father did—
like he was an idiot. He shook his head and patted back
his slicked down comb-over to make sure a hair hadn't
fallen out of place. Maybe the guy should have followed
Fenwick's example and just gotten a toupee.

"Before you do anything," the lawyer said, "you need
a paternity test to confirm the child is yours."

Blake shook his head.

"You need that test to see whether or not she's yours—
not just because of the money but for custody reasons."

"What do you mean?" He had no intention of taking the child away from her mother. He was doing everything within his power to make sure they weren't
separated.

"If she is yours, this woman denied you years of your daughter's life."

Blake flinched at the reminder. He'd been trying to let that resentment go. He didn't need to rehash it now. "That's the past. I can't change that," he said.

"You can take those years back," the lawyer insisted. "You can take the kid away from her."

Blake snorted. "How?" Juliette was not an unfit mother. The lawyer was insane. This meeting had been a mistake. He'd known it from the moment he'd opened the door to him.

"Why?" another voice asked.

The lawyer whirled around, and Blake saw Juliette standing behind him. She must have slipped silently into the suite while they'd been talking. How much had she heard?

Obviously enough that she looked furious.

"Why would you try to take my daughter away from me?" She wasn't asking the lawyer, though. She was asking Blake.

"I wouldn't," Blake assured her. "I can't."

But she was too angry to listen. He could see that now.

"I will fight you!" she said. And she turned toward the lawyer now. "You won't take my child away."

"If you didn't want to risk losing her, you shouldn't have tried to pass her off as a Colton," the man replied.

And Blake saw what Juliette always did—the snobbishness that made her think she was not in his league. He hoped like hell he had never acted that way—the way his father and his father's friend acted.

Superior.

Arrogant.

Juliette must have been too angry to speak. She just shook her head, turned and ran from the suite—slamming the door behind herself.

"Get the hell out of here!" Blake told the lawyer. But he was already heading to the door and opening it for himself. "I wouldn't have you represent me if you were the last lawyer in Red Ridge!"

Leaving the slime bag attorney to show himself out, Blake hurried out into the hall, but he caught no sight of Juliette or the bodyguards.

She was gone.

*She's gone.*

Not just her little kid who'd disappeared after going to the police station after the park that day. But now the K9 cop had disappeared, as well.

Where the hell had she gone?

Into hiding with her daughter?

He'd thought she was too proud and stubborn to do that. He'd been counting on her being too proud and stubborn to go into hiding. But a couple of days had passed with no sign of her.

She hadn't gone back to her house. The front windows were boarded up like it had been abandoned after the shooting. Too bad that damn mutt had alerted her to his presence that night. He might have been able to hit her if she hadn't ducked down so quickly. Then she'd returned fire, which had made him duck and miss again.

That dog was a pain in the ass. Literally. It had bit him when he'd been running away.

He should have done more than kick it after he'd shaken it loose. He should have shot the damn thing. But maybe he'd kicked it hard enough that it had been seriously injured.

Maybe that was why he hadn't seen her working.

But that still didn't explain where she'd gone.

She wasn't staying at the Colton Plaza Hotel, either. The suite on the twenty-first floor had only had one occupant the past couple of nights.

Blake Colton, billionaire businessman.

He was the guy who'd hired those damn security guards to protect her. But as if that wasn't bad enough, he kept getting in his way himself.

What the hell was some billionaire trying to play bodyguard for?

The K9 cop must be important to him.

Blake Colton must not mean much to her, though, since Juliette Walsh hadn't been to the hotel.

But he hadn't seen her anywhere around Red Ridge. Maybe she'd taken her daughter and left town.

Since he'd taken care of their last problem, his bosses were trying again to get him to leave town—before he got caught. They did not appreciate how good he was.

Nobody had ever caught him, and nobody would— because he didn't leave witnesses alive.

He had to find the woman and her daughter. He had to get rid of them for good.

# *Chapter 19*

Finn stood at the podium at the front of the briefing room, staring out at his officers. They all looked as frustrated as he felt. Too much time had passed with too few leads. On the Groom Killer and on the killer after Juliette and her daughter. Maybe the killers had both left town.

The thought didn't give him any relief, though. He didn't want them gone from Red Ridge. He wanted them gone—permanently. Locked up behind bars for the rest of their miserable lives—for the lives they'd taken.

Until the Groom Killer was caught, nobody in Red Ridge would feel safe getting married. Including Darby…

She was too worried about him to marry him. She

loved him too much. And he loved her too much to go long before making her his bride.

They had to catch that killer and soon.

The same for the park killer. The thought of a child being in danger was keeping Finn awake at night even more than his late-night visits and calls.

At least Red Ridge PD had some additional manpower now. "Let me introduce the newest member of our team, West Brand. He's on loan from our neighboring Wexton County's K9 unit while Dean Landon continues to recover from his gunshot wound."

The dark-haired man raised his hand in a slight wave at his new coworkers. Red Ridge PD was a close-knit group. They didn't readily welcome outsiders. So they didn't greet him any more warmly than he had them.

"His dog, Tam Lin—" Finn continued, gesturing to the Labrador sitting next to the new officer "—specializes in explosives detection."

Like Dean's dog did. Hopefully West could help fill the void in the department since Dean had been shot.

"Now let's get out there," Finn said. "And be careful…" He didn't want to lose anyone else. Before Juliette could leave the room, he called out, "Walsh…"

She stopped, Sasha at her side. "Yes, Chief?"

He waited until everyone else filed out of the briefing room. Then he asked, "Are you sure you're ready to go back out there?"

"I was never not ready," she said. "Dr. Colton wanted Sasha to take it easy for a couple of days."

Finn should have had his cousin, the vet, suggest the dog take longer to recover. Even though he'd been shorthanded the past couple of days, he preferred that to having to worry about Juliette.

And Blake...

Something must have happened between them, because she had insisted he not join her and Pandora at the safe house, where she'd spent the past two days.

"I'm not sure it's a good idea to put you back out there," he said. "We have Brand now—"

"You still need me and Sasha," she said. "She's the best drug-sniffing dog on the force."

He couldn't deny that. And he couldn't deny that there were too many drugs in the city. While they managed to apprehend some of the users and small-time dealers, they hadn't been able to get the suppliers at the top. Even though he had a pretty good idea who they were...

"Why don't you want me back at work?" she asked, her blue eyes narrowed with suspicion. "Did Blake get to you?"

He shook his head, though he couldn't deny that his cousin had tried. "No. It's been quiet the past two days—no more shootings. Everybody's better off with you in the safe house."

She flinched. "I can't stay hidden forever," she said. "I have a job, a life..." Her throat moved as if she was choking on emotion. But she fought it back to continue, "...a daughter. I want to know she'll always be safe. And the only way to do that is to catch that killer."

He nodded but cautioned, "There's no way to always keep her safe, though. There are other dangers than this killer out there."

"I know," she agreed with a heavy sigh as if she was already aware of another danger. "Can Sasha and I leave now? We need to check the airport."

He nodded in reluctant agreement. He'd put an extra car on her. But not Brand. Not yet...

He wanted the team he knew and trusted. He wasn't sure yet what to make of the new guy. He was going to have to look into him a little bit more...

Juliette had spent the past two days trying to keep her daughter safe. That was why she'd refused to let Blake visit. Let him sue her for custody if he wanted.

As he'd pointed out to her, the Coltons' reputation wasn't the greatest. She could beat him in court...if she could afford a lawyer.

*Damn him...*

He was following her, too—along with another patrol car and those bodyguards. She didn't see the bodyguards, but she knew they were there because she hadn't tried to lose anyone this time.

She glanced at Sasha. The beagle was bright-eyed and bursting with energy. She couldn't wait to get back to work. The rest had done her good.

Juliette hadn't been able to rest. She hadn't slept well without Blake's arm around her. Hadn't slept well with worrying that she might lose her daughter...

Would Blake try to take her?

He'd claimed that he wouldn't. But she hadn't let him say any more after his lawyer had insulted her. What a sleaze...

She pulled her car into the parking lot at the airport

and drew in a deep breath. She couldn't be distracted now. She had to stay focused on her job. Her life and Sasha's depended on it. The airport was small with limited flights, just commuter planes going to bigger airports in the vicinity. Because of that, the security was minimal, which made it a great place for dealers to try to run drugs.

"Come on, Sasha," Juliette said as she unclipped the dog from her harness. The beagle was so eager to do her job that she immediately started toward the building.

The tightness in Juliette's chest eased somewhat, too. At least with this, she knew what she was doing.

With Blake, she had no idea. His sister wanted her to cut him loose for his safety. What about hers? She was the one in danger from him—of losing everything. Her daughter and her heart...

She shook her head, forcing herself to focus. If she didn't, she might lose her life, too. Because she had no doubt the killer was probably out there—waiting for another chance to try for her.

Dante and Flash backed her up, walking through the airport in tandem with her and Sasha. She knew her fellow officer wasn't looking for someone running drugs, but for the killer. The murderer never got close, though—except for that night in her house and in the stairwell at the hotel. He'd been close then, and at the park when she'd seen him after Pandora had witnessed the murder.

She shivered as she remembered the cold look in his eyes. That look was so different than the one in the eyes of the people she busted for drugs. They looked desperate. Scared. He had been frighteningly calm. And determined…

As she and Sasha moved through the crowd, she noticed one of those desperate-looking people. The teenager carried a duffel bag. When she and Sasha drew closer, he shifted it to his other hand—as if that small distance would make Sasha unable to sniff the contents of it.

Juliette quickened her pace to close the distance between them, and Sasha tensed, starting to react. The beagle knew what was in that bag.

The teenager began to walk faster. But the terminal was small. With her on one side and Dante on the other, he really had nowhere to go.

"Stop!" she called out to him.

He hurried up instead—heading toward the men's room. As if that would keep her out…

He probably intended to flush his drugs.

"Stop!" she yelled again.

Dante and Flash had stepped between him and the bathroom. So he stopped and turned back toward her.

And in addition to that look of desperation in his eyes, there was one of fear. He looked so damn scared.

But Juliette wanted to scare him more; she wanted to scare him into telling her what every other drug dealer and user in this town was reluctant to do.

Who the hell was the shooter?

"What do you have in that bag?" she asked.

"I don't know." He dropped it to the floor. And Sasha was immediately on it, her nose pressed to the ratty canvas. "It's not mine," he said. "I was holding it for a friend."

"Let's go down to the police department and talk about your friends," she said. Turning him back around, she snapped cuffs over his bony wrists. He was young, yet old enough to talk without a parent present. Maybe he was even in his mid-twenties. Up close he looked older than she'd originally thought, so she didn't feel too bad about making him even more scared than he already was.

"You know," she mused as she led him toward the exit while Mancuso picked up the bag, "The last time I was trying to arrest someone, they got shot."

The kid arched his head around to look at her. "You shot 'im?"

She shook her head. "Nope, someone else did. Someone who didn't want that person to talk."

She stopped before pushing open the door to the parking lot. "Maybe we should talk now…before we go out there."

His throat moved, his Adam's apple bobbing up and down as he choked on his fear. "I—I have nothing to say…without my lawyer."

He was definitely older than she'd thought. Old and experienced enough to want a lawyer.

She pressed her hand against the glass of the door. "If you're sure…"

"Nobody wants *me* dead," he said.

She wished she could say the same about herself. And it was almost as if he knew that she couldn't— that he knew who she was and that she'd been targeted.

"Are you sure about that?" she asked. "You sure you don't want to talk to me?"

"I got nothing to say about nothing…"

She doubted that. This killer had taken out two dealers in Red Ridge. So other dealers and even some of their users had to know something about him.

"Okay…" But she hesitated a moment before stepping out into the lot.

There were hangars for private planes close to the airport. Roofs where the killer could go for the vantage point he liked to take his shots from.

She pushed open the door and advised him, "Keep low…"

But she was worried—even as Dante came up beside her. He nodded at her to go. She drew in a deep breath before stepping outside.

She didn't want the kid to get shot, or Dante. And she sure as hell didn't want to get shot. Then she made the mistake of glancing into the parking lot. And she saw Blake standing there—out of his car, watching her.

His sister was right. She needed to cut him loose— needed to make sure that he stopped following her around and putting his life in danger. She didn't want him to try to take Pandora from her.

But she didn't want him dead or injured, either.

Blake was so damn glad to see her again. He'd missed her the past couple of days. But she'd refused to see him at the safe house.

He could have just shown up since the bodyguards working for him knew where it was. But he hadn't wanted to cause a scene that might upset her and Pandora. With the killer's threats hanging over their heads, they were upset enough.

And the last thing he wanted was to upset his daughter. So there was no way he would ever try to take her from her mother. Juliette should know that. But she wouldn't let him explain that meeting with the lawyer.

She had refused to talk to him as well as see him. And he couldn't talk to her now. She was busy, bringing in another suspect.

And he remembered what had happened last time— at the bus terminal. It wasn't safe for her to be out here. Surely she knew that.

Why did she keep putting herself in danger?

It was about more than just doing her job, though. It was about Pandora, too. About taking the killer off the streets to protect the little girl.

But the killer did not share Blake's reluctance to separate mother and daughter. He had no such qualms about taking away the little girl's mother.

And just as Blake had feared, shots rang out again.

And just like at the bus terminal, Juliette dropped to the asphalt. Unlike that day, though, she was on top of the teenager she'd had in handcuffs. She was using her body to shield his.

She would have had to take a bullet for him.

# Chapter 20

The shots hadn't been close at all. But Juliette hadn't told the crying teenager that. She'd let him believe she'd saved his life back at the airport. And since bringing him to RRPD, she hadn't bothered to assuage his fears yet.

Blake's bodyguards had covered all the rooftops close to the airport, so the killer hadn't been able to get within range for a bullet to actually hit her or her suspect this time. No matter how angry she was with him, she couldn't deny that Blake had saved her life many times—personally and with that security agency he'd hired to protect her and their daughter.

While she appreciated that—or maybe because she appreciated that—she needed to talk to him. He'd been so worried at the airport, so scared that she'd been hit.

Juliette needed to make him back off, to keep him

away from the danger and herself. Just as she'd known five years ago, they were too different. They had no future together—besides coparenting their daughter. And she wasn't sure he really even wanted to do that.

But she couldn't think about him now. She couldn't think about anything but getting this kid to talk. Fortunately, because he thought she'd saved his life, he'd agreed to speak to her without a lawyer now.

"He tried to kill you," she told him as she settled onto the chair across the table from him.

The room was small and stark with just plain concrete block walls. There was a solid steel door behind the kid, and a mirror on the wall behind Juliette's head. She knew the chief stood behind that mirror, probably with Carson Gage. The detective and the boss knew she was the right one to question the kid, though.

Getting shot at together, her seemingly saving his life, had forged a bond between them. One she intended to exploit. "He's no friend of yours…"

"I don't know who *he* is," the young man said. His hands were cuffed to the table, so he had to lean forward to wipe away the tears that had leaked from his eyes. A strand of greasy black hair flopped over into his face. He blew it away and said, "I don't know who you're talking about."

"He's a hired assassin, right? Hired to take out the dealers who've been skimming from your boss or bosses." Everyone thought the Larson twins were behind the drug problem in Red Ridge. But the RRPD hadn't been able to prove it—despite having them under surveillance.

Was that why the killer had looked familiar to her even though he'd never been arrested? Had she seen him one of the times she'd been doing surveillance on the Larson twins?

"I work at a fast food place, lady," the young man replied. "I don't know what you're talking about…"

She shook her head. "The drugs in your duffel bag— there was too much for your personal use." He was likely a dealer working for the Larson twins. But Red Ridge PD hadn't been able to get any evidence against them because they probably hired people to clean up after them. People like the man from the park…

She rose from the chair. "It's fine if you don't want to help yourself. We've got enough to put you away for a long time…"

The room was small, so she was already at the door, reaching for the knob, when he called her back. "Wait, wait, wait!"

She paused, hesitated for a long moment before turning back toward him. "What?"

"What if I give you something?" he asked. "Could you make that stuff go away?"

"Are you bribing me?" The kid really was an idiot.

He shook his head. "No, no…not that. If I give you some information…"

"About him?"

"I told you I don't know who you're talking about…"

And she was beginning to believe him. She uttered a weary sigh before asking, "What have you got?"

"Do we have a deal?"

"I need to know what you're offering," she said.

"A big shipment," he said. "It's coming in on Friday at midnight…"

She lifted her shoulders in a shrug. "We'll have to see how big. Where's it coming in?"

He paused for a long moment, as if trying to determine if he could trust her. "Train station…"

On the midnight train…

It made sense—more sense than this kid trying to move drugs through the airport during the day.

She turned for the door again.

"Where are you going?" he asked. "Do we have a deal or not?"

"I'm not the one who makes deals," she said. "That'll be up to the district attorney's office." She'd already booked the kid on possession with suspicion of distributing. Someone would be picking him up soon to bring him to jail. She stepped out and closed the door behind herself.

And found the chief and Carson waiting for her in the hall. "Good work," Finn Colton praised her.

Carson nodded in agreement.

She felt no pride, though. She'd gotten some information out of him. But it wasn't the information she wanted. She was no closer to finding the man who was trying to kill her and her daughter.

"You'll be working that midnight shift," Finn told her.

She nodded, knowing he needed her and Sasha to find the shipment. Maybe whoever was bringing it in was high enough in the drug organization to know who the killer was. It wasn't a direct lead to him. But it might bring her closer to finally ending this nightmare.

First, she had to end something else, though.

Blake was shocked to open the hotel door to Juliette. After she'd overheard the conversation with the lawyer a few days before, he'd thought she might never come back.

She held out one of the room key cards to him. "I took this that morning…"

She'd snuck out of his arms, out of his bed…

His arms ached to hold her again, and his body ached for hers. She looked beautiful—as always. Tonight she wore some kind of loose dress. It was short and showed off her toned legs. He wanted to pick her up and carry her off to the bedroom. They never argued there.

But he knew they were about to argue. She'd been too furious that day she'd stormed out of here—too furious to give him a chance to explain before now. Not wanting to lose that chance, he rushed into his explanation. "That was not my lawyer," he said. "That was my father's lawyer."

But Blake never should have agreed to take the meeting with him.

"It doesn't matter," she said.

"Yes, it does," he replied. "The guy's an ass."

"He's right about the paternity test," she said. "You will need one—especially if you have any intention of fighting me for custody."

"I don't!" he assured her.

"That's good," she said, "because you'd lose. And I know you hate to lose."

He did. That was why he didn't want to lose her.

"I would never try to take you from your daughter," he said. "That's why I've been following you around, making sure nothing happens to you."

"For her sake?" she asked, and her body was tense, as if she was bracing herself for a blow.

"Yours too," he said. "I don't want anything to happen to you. That's why I think you should quit your job."

Her blue eyes widened with shock. "What?"

"I'm rich," he said. "I can support you and Pandora. You don't need to work. I can take the two of you out of the country—back to one of my places in Singapore or London or Hong Kong."

The color had drained from Juliette's face, leaving her pale but for the dark circles beneath her eyes. "You don't know me at all," she murmured.

"Of course I know you," he said. "I know that you're a good mother who wants what's best for her daughter. This is what's best. You quitting the Red Ridge PD."

She gasped. "I've worked my whole life. And you just expect me to stop?"

"You don't have to work so hard anymore," he said. "I will take care of you and our daughter."

She shook her head. "I won't be your mistress."

He chuckled. "You won't be my mistress. I'm not married." But maybe he should be…then he wouldn't have to worry so much about her and Pandora. He could always be with them.

He waited for the panic he'd felt that day he'd carried Juliette over the threshold to this suite. But it didn't come. Yet...

"I won't be a kept woman," she said with a shudder. "Then your father and his sleazy lawyer will be right to think I'm some kind of opportunist."

He snorted. "If you were an opportunist, you would have told me when you found out you were pregnant. You would have wanted me to financially support you." Instead of fighting him over it...

"You just made this a whole hell of a lot easier," she murmured.

And he tensed now. "What?"

"I came here to tell you it's over..." She shrugged. "Whatever it was...whatever we were doing...it's over... I don't want to see you anymore."

She'd made that pretty clear the past couple of days. But he'd thought she'd just needed to calm down after that horrible conversation she'd overheard.

"If you're still mad about the lawyer, I told you he's not working for me," Blake assured her. "I'm not going after custody..."

"Just leave us alone," she implored him. "You told me five years ago that you had no intention of ever being a husband or a father. So stick with that. Don't make the mistakes your father made."

He flinched as she struck that nerve he'd exposed to her so long ago. "Now you don't want me in her life?"

"Not if you're going to hurt and disappoint her," she said. "And you will when you leave Red Ridge and focus on your business again. So just go now—before she gets any more attached."

"What about you?" he asked. "Are you attached?"

Color rushed back into her face. But she shook her head. "No. No, I'm not…"

"You don't want me?" he asked. He stepped closer, hoping to call her bluff. But what if she wasn't bluffing?

What if she really didn't care about him?

He pressed his lips to hers. But she didn't move. She didn't kiss him back as he brushed his mouth over hers. Then finally she gasped, and her lips parted on a moan.

She was bluffing.

But why?

"So you met her?" Fenwick asked Patience the minute she stepped into his den at home.

"She's a K9 cop, so I already know her," his daughter replied.

"Did you know she had your brother's kid?" His hand trembled on his liquor glass when he thought of it, thought of being a grandfather.

No. It wasn't possible.

"Of course not," she said. "I just found out myself."

"How could she have kept this secret for so long?" Fenwick wondered. Especially if she was after the Colton money. Had she just been waiting for Blake to be as successful as he was now? Until he'd become a billionaire?

Patience shrugged. "She didn't think he wanted to be a father."

Fenwick flinched. He knew why. Blake didn't want to be like him. But in staying away from his kid, he was acting more like him than not. Fenwick knew he'd never paid enough attention to his children—especially Blake.

He'd been busy. He'd provided for them, though.

Until now...

Now his livelihood was being threatened. Hell, his entire life was being threatened—if he lost his business. But for some reason he wasn't as worried about the business as he was Blake.

"You don't think he's going to do something stupid like propose to her?" he asked, speaking his greatest fear aloud.

He knew how grooms wound up in Red Ridge. Shot through the heart with a cummerbund stuffed down their throats. He grimaced as the image of his handsome son as the Groom Killer's next victim flashed through his head.

"Even if he does..." Patience began.

And Fenwick's heart stopped beating for a moment. His sister—who'd admitted to seeing them together—must have considered it a possibility.

"I don't think she'd accept," Patience continued.

Fenwick shook his head. "She'd be a fool to turn down a proposal from a billionaire."

"She would be in love with him," Patience said. "And I think she might be. She doesn't want Blake getting hurt any more than we do."

Fenwick should have been relieved, but he knew his son too well. Blake was a billionaire because he worked hard and stopped at nothing to get what he wanted.

If he wanted Juliette Walsh, there was no way she

would turn him down. The only reason they probably wouldn't wind up married was if Blake got killed.

And that was just too great a possibility.

# Chapter 21

Juliette was supposed to be cutting him loose—not clutching him closer. But once Blake had kissed her, she'd lost all control. The passion between them burned too brightly, too hot to be denied. She had tried to keep her lips still beneath his—had tried to resist.

But her pulse had quickened, her skin had tingled, and her heart had begun to pound so fiercely—that she couldn't fight it anymore. She cared too much about him.

So she would make him leave her alone.

Just not yet.

She gripped his shoulders as he lifted and carried her. He didn't carry her to the bedroom, though—just to the couch. He sat down with her straddling his lap, and he tugged her dress up and over her head. It dropped to the floor behind her. Then her bra quickly followed. It wasn't as if anyone else could see them on the twenty-first floor. No other building in Red Ridge was as tall as the Colton Plaza Hotel.

He held her breasts, cupping and massaging them while brushing his palms over the taut nipples. She moaned again at the sensations racing through her. She needed him. Now.

So she dragged off his shirt and tossed it aside before reaching for the button of his jeans. He caught her hand, though. Then he lifted her and stood. He undid his jeans and kicked them off. But he leaned over and pulled a condom from the pocket. He must have been as desperate to be with her as she was to be with him, because he sheathed himself quickly.

Then he sat back down.

Before she straddled his lap again, she pulled off her panties. His hand moved between her legs, stroking over her mound as he made sure she was ready for him.

She was more than ready. She was about to go out of her mind with the tension winding so tightly inside her. It had been only a couple of days since they'd made love. But it felt like it had been years again.

How was she going to give him up forever?

She had to be selfless—for his sake.

To keep him safe…

He pulled her down onto his lap, carefully guiding his shaft inside her. She adjusted and arched, taking him deeper. He felt so damn good—filled her so perfectly.

They moved perfectly together, too, in absolute unison. They were in sync like soul mates.

But Blake was not her soul mate. While he understood how to please her physically, he had no idea how to please her emotionally. It was probably because he'd never been given love that he didn't know how to give it—to her or to their daughter. So she would take only what he could give her now—the physical pleasure.

His hands moved over her breasts again, stroking, caressing...

And his mouth mated with hers, their kisses hungry and intense. Their lips clung, their tongues tangled—their kisses alone brought her to the first peak of pleasure.

Then he thrust harder and moved faster, and another orgasm overcame her, making her body shudder with the intensity of it.

He moved her then, so that he was on top, she lying on the cushions. He made love to her all over again, lifting her legs high as he thrust inside her. And she came again...

Then he tensed and groaned as he joined her in ecstasy. "That was incredible," he murmured.

It was goodbye. But before she could tell him that, he slipped away from her, and she heard water running in the bathroom.

She needed to get dressed and get out of there. But she felt too boneless, too satiated, to move. She forced some strength into her limbs, though, and rose from the couch. She'd just pulled her dress back over her head when he reappeared. All he wore were his jeans, low on his lean hips.

She wanted him all over again.

Then he spoke. "See how good this could be for

us? You don't need to work. You and Pandora can live with me."

And suddenly she felt sick rather than satiated. He had just cheapened what they'd done, making it sound like an arrangement rather than a relationship. She shook her head. "I told you I won't be your mistress."

"That's not what I'm saying," he said. "I want to take care of you and Pandora."

"You want to take us away from Red Ridge," she said. "This is our home. We're not going anywhere—especially not with you."

He reached out. "Juliette, you're blowing this out of proportion—"

"I was already trying to tell you that this isn't working," she reminded him. "That we have no future—"

"We have a daughter."

"You need to get your paternity test to prove that." Maybe she could tie him up in court or bluff him into walking away from them.

But the last time she'd tried bluffing—about her attraction to him—he'd called her on it. He'd proved that he affected her.

Too much. But not anymore. All he'd offered her was money and sex. Not his heart.

She wanted his heart. But even if he'd offered it, she might have refused—for his safety. Because she cared more about him than herself. He had her heart. He'd probably had it since that night nearly five years ago.

"What's going on, Juliette?" he asked, his brow furrowed with confusion.

He probably wasn't used to not getting what he

wanted. But she had yet to stop working no matter how many times he'd asked her to go into hiding with Pandora. So he should have been accustomed to her not giving him what he asked for.

"If you want to see Pandora again, you better get that lawyer back," she said, "because I'm not going to let you see her."

"What? Why not?"

"Just go back to London or Milan or wherever you call home," she said. "I don't want you here. Pandora and I don't need you."

He flinched as if she'd hurt him. But then he shook his head, stubbornly unwilling to believe her. "Liar," he said.

She didn't argue with him. She just hurried out of the suite. For the last time…

She was not coming back. She had to let whatever was between her and Blake Colton go. She had to let him go.

She was lying. Wasn't she?

Blake had been asking himself that question for the past couple of days. But she had not come to his suite again. She had also stuck by her decision to not let him see Pandora anymore. Was it to protect the little girl, though?

Or to protect him?

"She what?" he asked Finn. The police chief had called him to this meeting in his office at the Red Ridge Police Department.

"She threatened to take out a restraining order

against you," the chief said. "She wants you to stop following her around."

He shook his head. "I'm not going to stop."

"She agreed to keep the bodyguards," Finn divulged. "She just doesn't want you."

He was getting that message loud and clear. But what was her motivation?

Was she still furious with him over what the lawyer had said and over what he'd said? He'd denied wanting her to be his mistress. But maybe he did want her to be a kept woman. He wanted to keep her.

But could he trust her?

She had already kept his daughter from him for nearly five years. And now she was trying to do that again. But he wouldn't let her get away with it this time. He was going to have to hire a lawyer and get that paternity test. He would fight her for visitation.

He would fight her on this, too.

"Why not?"

"You're not a bodyguard," Finn said. "You're not a cop. I never should have allowed you to follow her around in the first place."

Blake bristled like Sasha when she caught the scent of drugs. "You didn't allow me to do anything. I can follow her around. I'm not threatening her. I'm trying to keep her safe. No judge in Red Ridge is going to grant her a restraining order."

Finn snorted. "Because you're Fenwick Colton's kid."

Blake bristled some more. It was as if Finn was deliberately trying to piss him off. "I don't know what you're trying to do," he told his cousin, "but you're not going to be able to keep me away."

"Damn it, Blake," Finn said. "You're going to get yourself killed if you keep intervening in police business."

"I haven't gotten hurt yet," he said.

Finn pointed toward his face. But his argument was weak. The scratch had faded and all but disappeared.

He shook his head. "What's the deal? What's really going on?"

With Finn and with Juliette. She'd acted so strangely that night in his suite.

"She flipped that kid from the airport and got him to inform on a shipment coming into the train station on Friday," Finn said. "It's big. She can't be distracted. You can't get in her way."

Panic pressed down on Blake's lungs, stealing his breath away. He had a bad feeling—a very bad feeling about this.

"You need to bring in someone else," he said. He'd heard there was a new K9 cop on loan from some other county. "Use the new guy."

Finn shook his head. "His specialty is explosives. Juliette's is narcotics. She and Sasha are the best," her boss said with pride.

Blake felt a flash of pride, too, and he understood a little bit why Juliette had been so reluctant to quit her job. She didn't just enjoy it; she was damn good at it.

Finn continued, "So no matter what you say, I'm not taking her off this assignment. I need her."

So did Blake. And he had a feeling that if she went to make that bust, he would lose her forever.

But then, he'd never really had her to begin with. They'd had only that magical night so long ago and a few stolen moments since he'd returned to Red Ridge. But if this assignment was as dangerous as Blake felt it was, he might never get the chance for any more moments with her.

She'd taken the bait—just as he'd planned. He'd had no intention of shooting that kid—even if he had been able to get close enough.

But those damn bodyguards had been in his way.

As usual...

If they hadn't been covering all the buildings close enough to the airport for him to get an accurate shot, he might have taken a chance.

Maybe he could have ended this—and her—already. He was getting sick of Red Ridge. It was long past time that he ended this.

Once she was dead, there would be a funeral. Her kid would have to attend. And then she would join her mother—in death.

Just as he'd promised them that day in park. They were going to die.

Juliette Walsh was going to get one hell of a surprise when she showed up at the train station to make her big bust. She was going to get a bullet in her brain. And whoever else got in his way—the bodyguards, the other cops or that rich guy who'd been following her around like her damn dog—was going to wind up dead, too.

# Chapter 22

Juliette was in plain clothes for the morning briefing. She wasn't staying. Her shift wouldn't start until later, so that she and Sasha would be fresh for the midnight train coming into Red Ridge station.

Would there really be a shipment of drugs on it? Or had the kid just been trying to get out of trouble?

Juliette wasn't sure if she should have believed him. But he'd been so upset at nearly getting shot that he'd seemed sincere. Hopefully whoever was bringing in those drugs knew about the man from the park. She had to find him. Had to stop him...

Pandora was so sick of the safe house. She wanted to go home. And so did Juliette.

The little girl also wanted Blake.

And so did Juliette...

But this was for the best—for all of them. While he wanted to protect Juliette, he didn't love her. It didn't sound like his father had ever been able to show love—at least not to his kids.

Was that how Blake was going to be?

If he couldn't show love to Pandora, Juliette would rather not have him around the little girl. Or around her...

And it was better for him this way, too. He wouldn't be in danger anymore.

But when the chief stepped up to the podium to begin the morning briefing, he met her gaze and shook his head. And she knew...

He hadn't been able to threaten or coerce Blake to stop following her around. That was not good. She didn't want him at the drug bust tonight.

She just had an odd feeling about it all, like something wasn't quite right. Like maybe it had been too easy...

"As some of you know, Officer Walsh got a tip that there will be a big shipment of drugs coming into Red Ridge tonight on the midnight train. We're going to be careful to stay out of sight until the train pulls in. Walsh will be there with Sasha. Detective Gage will be backing her up along with Officer West Brand."

Brand. She glanced over at the officer on loan from Wexton County. She had an odd feeling about him, as well. Since he'd started, he'd kept to himself—even when working with everybody else. He didn't volunteer any information about himself, and he gave only vague answers to the questions people asked. He seemed secretive, like he had something to hide.

Yet who was she to talk? She'd kept her child's paternity a secret for over four years. But her secret hadn't affected anyone else.

Except Blake...

After she'd kept that secret from him—his daughter from him—she was surprised that he wanted to protect her at all. But she wasn't naive enough to believe he'd forgiven her or that he would ever trust her. That might have been why all he had offered her was his protection.

Not his heart.

He didn't trust her with it. And she couldn't blame him after her betrayal. Now she was keeping her daughter from him all over again—threatening that he'd have to call a lawyer and go to court to demand the rights she should have given him when Pandora was born.

Lost in her own thoughts, she hadn't realized that everyone else had left until the chief stopped next to her chair.

"Are you sure you're up for this?" he asked.

She uttered a weary sigh. Except for that night she'd slept in Blake's arms, she hadn't had much sleep since that day in the park. Heck, she hadn't had much sleep when she'd heard he was back in town. She'd been scared to see him again. "I'd feel better if you had managed to get Blake to back off. The threat of the restraining order didn't work?"

He shook his head. "How would it? He knows no judge would give it to you. He hasn't threatened you. Instead he's been trying to protect you."

Frustration gripped Juliette. Why was he so damn stubborn? Must have been the Colton in him. But she couldn't say that in front of her boss, who was also a Colton. "I don't need his protection."

"I know," Finn said. "We've got this. Gage and Brand will have your back. And I'm sure those bodyguards will be close, too."

"Are you sure about Brand?" she asked.

Finn's usually open face shuttered, and he looked away from her. "Of course. Why wouldn't I be sure about him?"

"What do you know about him?"

"He's an explosives specialist," the chief said. "He's good."

That told her what he did. Not who he was. Not anything about his character. "But is he trustworthy?" she asked.

"Beyond reproach," Finn insisted.

And that strange feeling she'd had about the temporary team member intensified. She'd thought he was keeping secrets. Now she suspected that the chief was, too, but that secret was about Brand.

Who the hell was he?

"So he'll have my back tonight?" she asked, needing assurances.

The chief nodded.

But she didn't feel reassured. She understood now how Blake must have felt when he'd learned the momentous secret she'd kept from him. She certainly didn't like being kept in the dark.

She just hoped that she wouldn't wind up there permanently.

* * *

Blake waited in the hall outside the briefing room. The receptionist had not wanted to let him past her. But when he'd turned on the charm, she'd relented and pointed him to a chair in the hall. She kept looking at him over the top of silver-framed glasses, though.

He'd watched everyone else file out of the briefing room—but for Juliette and the chief. Maybe Finn was talking her out of going to the bust.

He didn't think so. His cousin had definitely sounded as if he considered Juliette the best officer to follow up on the tip about the drug shipment. But every time she'd gone to the airport or the bus terminal, something had happened. She'd nearly been shot.

Blake didn't like her chances for surviving the train station.

The minute she stepped out of the room with Finn, he jumped up from his chair. She groaned when she saw him and just shook her head.

"Don't harass her," Finn warned him. "Or she might be able to get that restraining order yet."

"I would testify," the receptionist warned him, her dark brows arching into her bangs.

He didn't know if she was kidding or not. No one could seriously think he meant Juliette any harm. Could they?

Juliette walked away from him, toward the front doors of the police department. She stopped before she stepped out, though, and turned back to him. "I don't understand why you won't leave me alone."

"I told you that I'm doing this for Pandora," he said. "I don't want her to lose her mother."

She flinched as if the thought filled her with dread. Then why risk it?

"You hired the bodyguards," she said. "Let them do their job. Let me do my job. Stay out of my way. Stay out of my life, Blake."

A pang struck his heart, and he felt like she'd stabbed him. It was clear that she meant it now.

She continued, "You won't help out your dad with his financial problems because you're worried about your business. How can you leave it this long? Don't you need to go back to your offices?"

He could work anywhere. But that wasn't her point. And he knew it. "You really want to get rid of me," he mused. "Is that why you didn't let me know about Pandora? You don't want to share her?"

Her lips pressed together in a tight line, as if she was forcing herself to hold back some words. She glanced around them and shook her head. Then she murmured, "Not here..."

"Then where?" he asked. "You said you're not going back to my suite."

"I'm not."

She wasn't going to sleep with him again. Had he offended her that much when he'd offered to support her? He knew other women who would have been thrilled with that offer. But Juliette was fiercely independent. She'd been taking care of herself and everyone else in her life for a long time.

But he didn't know what else to offer her. Marriage? He doubted she wanted that; she'd been pointing out to him over and over again that they had nothing in common.

But they had something very important in common. Someone, actually.

Their daughter.

"Let me come see Pandora," he said.

"I told you—"

"I know—get a lawyer," he said. "I can—if you want me to…"

She pursed her lips again as to hold back some more words. And he wanted to kiss them. He wanted to kiss her so badly.

But she was right. Not here…

He wasn't giving up, though—on their daughter or on her. "Someone else can handle Sasha tonight," he said. "You don't have to go."

Her blue eyes widened with surprise that he knew about the shipment. Then she sighed. "Sasha is my partner. I'm going with her tonight."

Just as she didn't want her daughter getting hurt, she didn't want her dog getting hurt. Was that why she'd threatened him with the restraining order? Did she not want him to get hurt, either?

Was that why she kept pushing him away? For his own protection?

Before he could ask, she pushed open the doors and walked out of the department. He tensed, like he did every time she was out in the open. He expected bullets to fly, expected that psycho to shoot at her.

But nothing happened. She made it to her vehicle

without incident. And he released a breath of relief. She was safe for now.

But she wouldn't be tonight—not during that drug bust. She would be in danger then. That was why he had to be there. He had to try to save her from herself.

But who would save him from her?

Patience watched her brother as he paced her office. He'd always had more energy than she and their sisters did. That was why his mother had given full custody to their father. She hadn't wanted to deal with a hyper-active little boy.

But Blake hadn't exactly been hyperactive. He'd been hyperfocused. Once something had caught his interest, he'd focused all his attention on mastering it. Like football and basketball and golf and lacrosse…

Whatever sport he'd played in school he'd practiced incessantly. And when he'd gotten interested in business, it hadn't been enough for him to work for someone else—especially not their father. He'd had to build his own.

He wasn't the kind of person who delegated or hired people to carry out his orders. He had to be personally involved. He had to get his hands dirty.

Maybe that was why he persisted in following Juliette around. He didn't trust that she would be safe unless he was the one protecting her.

But Patience wondered and worried that there was more to it than that. "You love her," she said.

He abruptly stopped pacing. But he didn't turn to her.

It was as if he didn't want her to see his face—probably because his feelings were written all over it.

She should have been happy that he could feel—that he could care about someone else. That meant that he wasn't as much like their father as Patience had worried that he was. But she wasn't happy about that—because she was afraid that caring about Juliette Walsh might get him killed.

"You love her," she repeated.

He shook his head. "I don't know what love is," he remarked. "I've never seen my mom or dad in love. Lust, maybe, but not love…"

And maybe lust was all he'd thought he'd felt for Juliette. But Patience could tell his feelings went much deeper than attraction.

"We're not our parents," she said.

"I sure as hell hope not," he said.

And she could tell that it worried him, that he didn't want to be like their father.

"But what if I am?" he asked her. "Would it be better if I just walked away from her?"

"Juliette?"

"She hasn't given me a choice," he replied. "She wants nothing to do with me."

So she had cut him loose like Patience had suggested. She should have been relieved. But seeing the look on his face, the pain, she felt a horrible heaviness pressing on her heart. Guilt.

She probably should have kept her mouth shut.

"I'm talking about Pandora," he said. "Should I walk away from her? Is she better off without me in her life?"

Patience sighed. "Oh, Blake…"

What had she done?

She'd only wanted to keep her brother safe. She'd been so worried about his life, though, that she'd gotten his heart broken with her meddling. Maybe she was the one who was like their dad.

"I'm sorry," she murmured.

"It's not your fault," he said.

But he didn't know what she'd done. She'd opened her mouth to tell him when his cell rang.

He pulled it from his pocket and accepted the call without so much as a glance at her. It reminded her of how their father had always taken calls no matter what was going on—her recital, one of Blake's games…

If he'd bothered to show up at all, he'd been on his phone the entire time.

"Yes," he answered his caller. "I'll be there. Thanks…"

The call disconnected before he could say anything else.

"Business?" she asked.

He shook his head. "Juliette. She's letting me see Pandora tonight. Now I just have to figure out what's the right thing to do. If this should be the last time I see my daughter…"

Patience hoped it wouldn't be. But she was more worried about him losing his life than leaving the country.

## Chapter 23

She had been wrong—about so many things. Juliette realized that now as she watched Blake play with Pandora. Even though his father might not have been able to show him love, Blake could show fatherly love.

He obviously loved their daughter.

She had been a fool to keep them apart. Instead of being selfless, she'd been being selfish. Sure, she wanted him out of danger. Hell, with everything going on in Red Ridge right now, she would prefer he left the country.

But she should have never kept him apart from Pandora—not those first four years of her life and definitely not now that they'd met. They hadn't just met. They'd connected in a way that had Juliette experiencing feelings she wasn't proud of: jealousy, possessiveness.

She had always been her little girl's favorite person. But already Blake had come to mean so much to her. And it was obvious from the way he looked at her, the way he touched her hair and kissed her forehead, that she meant so much to him, too.

Juliette's heart ached just from watching them. Then it warmed and swelled as love replaced the jealousy. She loved them both so much. All she wanted was for them both to be happy. But she wasn't sure how she could make that happen or even if she could.

She couldn't do what Blake had asked; she couldn't give up her job and move away from Red Ridge with him—not even if he was offering more than a sexual relationship. She loved her job, her friends—this city. Red Ridge held the memories of her parents, and memories were all she had left of them now.

But he wasn't offering her more than a sexual relationship except for his protection. She didn't need that, either.

"Mommy! Mommy!" Pandora called out to her.

And she realized she'd been lost in her thoughts. She forced a smile. "What, sweetheart?"

"Sing me the song, sing me the song!" Pandora implored her. She was tucked into bed already.

Blake had supervised teeth brushing and had pulled up the covers while Juliette had just followed them around, watching them and yearning. If only Blake could love her like he loved their daughter, maybe they could have this life together—maybe they could become the family Pandora so obviously wanted them to be.

"Mommy has a special bedtime song she sings when I can't get to sleep."

Her face heated with embarrassment. Pandora must have been tone-deaf to appreciate her singing.

Blake's lips curved into a grin. "Really? Mommy sings?"

"I'm surprised it doesn't give her nightmares," she admitted.

When he chuckled, her heart flipped. She had fallen for him—so hard. That must have been the reason for her jealousy. Not that she envied his love for their daughter but that she wanted some of it for herself, too.

"Sing, Mommy," Pandora demanded.

She was such an imp.

Juliette could deny her nothing. That was why she'd called Blake. Her daughter had wanted to see her daddy. She'd asked the past couple of nights as well, but Juliette had used the excuse that he was busy. But when she'd tried that tonight, Pandora had asked if he was too busy for her.

And Juliette's heart had cracked with her daughter's pain and her own guilt. That might be the case, someday, when Blake had to return to his businesses. But it wasn't now. She was the one who'd kept them apart.

Knowing that she deserved more than some embarrassment for what she'd done, Juliette began to sing. Her voice rose and fell, missing notes and cracking, as she sang "Twinkle, Twinkle, Little Star." It was so bad that Blake winced for her or maybe because she'd hurt his ears. But Pandora applauded.

Her daughter wasn't hard to please. Maybe she would

be okay with whatever time Blake could make for her around his business trips. Maybe they could figure something out to make Pandora happy.

But Juliette knew Blake couldn't make her happy—unless he was willing to give her his heart instead of just his protection.

"Now you, Daddy," Pandora urged him. "You sing now!"

"I'm not sure I know that one," he said, obviously stalling.

"Everybody knows 'Twinkle, Twinkle,'" Pandora said, as if he was an idiot. She was already a master manipulator at four years old.

Beneath his breath, he murmured, "You are my father's granddaughter…persistent…"

So he'd recognized the manipulation, as well. But he caved for it, probably so that he wouldn't feel like an idiot, and began to sing. Of course his voice was perfect, just like everything else about him.

Instead of clapping, though, Pandora began to snore. Blake had managed to make the song sound like the lullaby it was intended to be.

"She's not going to ask for me to sing that again," she remarked as she pulled the light blanket to the little girl's chin and kissed her forehead.

Blake leaned over the child to do the same, and he pressed his mouth to the exact same spot Juliette had kissed. Even though they didn't touch, she felt her lips begin to tingle.

She wanted him to kiss her.

She wanted him. But she wanted more than sex. She wanted this—this evening. Love. Family.

But he hadn't offered her that. And even if he had, she was in no position to accept it now. Not with a killer determined to get rid of her and their daughter. And if Blake were to propose, then a killer would try to get rid of him. A different killer—the Groom Killer—but one probably even more dangerous than the one after her.

She hurried out into the hall. She needed to dress in her uniform, needed to get Sasha and head to the train station soon. But she'd only made it outside Pandora's bedroom door when Blake grabbed her arm.

He whirled her around and pulled her close to him. And then he was kissing her.

Her hands slipped up to the nape of his neck, and she held him there for a long moment, kissing him back. But then she moved her hands to his shoulders and pushed him away. Panting for breath, she said, "I didn't call you here for that."

"I know. You called me here to talk me out of following you tonight," he said.

Heat rushed to her face. That had been one of her reasons. But Pandora was the biggest reason. She was always the biggest reason for everything Juliette did.

"Can I talk you out of it?" she asked.

"Only way I won't be there is if you're not," he said.

"Blake, this is a bad idea…"

"I agree," he said. "That's why I think you should stay here—with her—with us…" And he lowered his head and kissed her again.

She wanted to stay—so badly. But his coercion reminded her of that last night in his hotel suite. And she jerked away from him. "I will never be your kept woman," she said. "I have a job that I love. I'm not giving it up for you—to follow you around the world."

Not even if he loved her. But of course, he didn't. If he loved her, he would understand her—and how much her job meant to her. But he didn't even know her.

His voice a gruff whisper, he said, "Your job is dangerous enough when there isn't a killer after you. But there is one. You need to be extra careful now."

"I need to not be distracted," she said. "If something happens tonight, it'll be because of you—because you're in my way. You're the one who should stay here—with her."

"In case you don't come back?" he asked. "See, even you have a bad feeling about this."

She did. But she wasn't sure why. Maybe it was because she didn't entirely trust that the young dealer had been telling the truth. Or that she didn't entirely trust the new guy on loan from Wexton County.

The last thing she needed tonight was to worry about Blake, too. Most of her worry was about him, like maybe he was the one who was going to wind up getting hurt, and this time it would be more serious than a scratch on his handsome face.

She'd wanted to push him into going away—leaving the country. She knew she didn't really want to lose him. She loved him. But she couldn't tell him—not now—probably not even after the Groom Killer was caught.

Because if she confessed her love and he didn't return her feelings, she would be more embarrassed than she'd been singing in front of him. No. She would be worse than embarrassed; she would be crushed.

Maybe Blake should have listened to her. Maybe he shouldn't have shown up. If something happened because he'd distracted her, he would never forgive himself. And if Pandora ever learned he was to blame, she would never forgive him, either.

But he was being careful. From the bodyguards, he'd learned how to keep more to the shadows—how to make himself invisible. He wore a hat, the bill pulled low over his face, so that he wasn't recognizable.

Juliette knew he was there, though. She kept glancing at where he sat in the chairs. Had he made a huge mistake in following in her here?

It seemed as if he just kept making mistake after mistake with her. He kept offending her when he didn't mean to. All he wanted was to take care of her.

But to a woman like Juliette, one as fiercely independent and strong, he should have realized that was an insult. She didn't need taking care of.

What did she need?

Her daughter. Her job. The killer caught…

What about him? Did she need him?

She'd pushed him away easily enough tonight. But then she'd known she had to leave—that she'd had to come here—because of that tip.

Would she have pushed him away if she hadn't had to leave? Would she have pushed him away if he'd told her he was starting to fall for her?

His heart lurched as he realized that he already had.

Hell, he'd fallen for her nearly five years ago during that incredible evening they'd spent together. He'd never connected with anyone the way he had with her, and not just physically or sexually but emotionally, as well. He'd told her things he'd never shared with anyone else.

Somehow, something about her had compelled him to trust her with his innermost thoughts and feelings. But then, when he'd learned she wasn't who he'd thought she was that night and that she hadn't told him about his daughter, he'd lost that trust. And with that trust had gone his feelings for her.

But watching her with their daughter, watching her do her job…

He'd fallen for her all over again. And loving her was why he was so determined to keep her safe. Maybe if he'd told her that, she wouldn't have come here tonight.

But he doubted it. He doubted even his love could stop Juliette from doing her job. She loved it too much. And because he loved her, he never should have tried to get her to quit it. He should have supported her. Instead of trying to take her and Pandora away from Red Ridge, he should have told her he'd come back here—permanently.

Would any of that had made a difference to her? Would she have accepted his proposal?

What the hell had he done? He hadn't proposed. He hadn't asked her to marry him just to be available to him. No wonder she'd been insulted.

He'd made a mess of everything.

He needed to fix this. He glanced at his watch. It was too close to midnight to bother her now. He didn't want her distracted. He wanted her totally focused on her job, especially tonight.

He had such a bad feeling about this potential bust. The informant's tip was highly suspicious to him—that a user or some low-level dealer would know about a big shipment. Why would anyone have told him about it? It seemed like his boss would have worried that he'd either spill his guts or try to hijack the shipment.

But Blake knew nothing about drugs or police work. He did know about business, though, and that would have been like his telling the mailroom clerk about some electronics invention. He wouldn't have done it because he would have worried that the kid would blab.

It almost felt like someone had wanted this kid to blab. Why? To make sure that Juliette would be here? To set her up? Was this an ambush?

He looked around the train station. Nobody looked like him—like he was trying to disguise himself. And the killer would have had to be wearing a very good disguise, or Juliette would have already recognized him. She kept looking uneasily around the station. But maybe the guy was waiting for her outside like he had at the bus terminal and the airport.

The bodyguards had the surrounding buildings covered, though. They were also watching the parking lot for anyone driving up. The knot of apprehension in Blake's stomach eased somewhat. Nobody could get close enough to her for a bullet to strike her out there.

A distant whistle alerted him to the arrival of the train. Red Ridge was old-fashioned enough that their trains still had whistles. He glanced at his watch. A minute before midnight. There was the squeaking of brakes as the train began to slow down to stop at the terminal.

Juliette and Sasha stood near the doors through which everyone would enter the station. And that was when it struck him…

The only place he, the bodyguards and Juliette's fellow officers didn't have covered…

The train.

And with absolute certainty, Blake knew that it didn't carry any shipment of drugs. It carried the killer. He was going to get off the train.

Blake jumped up from his seat and leaped over travelers' bags to race across the station toward Juliette.

Her eyes widened with alarm as she saw him approaching. She'd told him to keep his distance. But he didn't care. He couldn't let her get shot.

"He's on the train!" Blake shouted.

And just as he did, the doors slid open and a man stepped through them. He hadn't seen him before. But he instinctively knew who he was. So did Sasha, because the beagle began to bark and snarl.

Blake jumped forward, diving toward Juliette. He needed to knock her down—needed to get her out of the line of fire. But in doing that, he put himself there— right before the shots rang out.

# Chapter 24

It all happened so quickly. Juliette had had no idea why Blake suddenly charged toward her. He was shouting but she'd only heard the last word of what he was saying, "Train!"

Then she'd realized what he already had. The killer was on the train.

She'd drawn her weapon, but before she could fire at the man who'd stepped through the doors, Blake had knocked her down. Shots rang out. People screamed and ran for their lives.

She pushed Blake off her and returned fire. The man darted back through the open doors and onto the platform. Sasha's leash had slipped from Juliette's hands, so the beagle tore out after him.

Juliette turned toward Blake, who lay on his side next to her. "Are you okay?" she asked.

His head jerked in a sharp nod. "Yeah, yeah! Are you?"

She nodded.

Then he urged her, "Go! Do your job. Get that son of a bitch!"

Love swelled her heart. He couldn't have said anything sweeter to her unless he'd professed his love. His confidence in her—in her abilities—was nearly as important to her as his loving her.

She rolled to her feet and rushed off after Sasha, letting her barking lead her past the train. He hadn't jumped back inside, but Brand was moving through the cars as if he had. He was wasting his time.

She signaled at him as she ran. But she didn't wait to see if he got off the train and followed her. She had to catch up to Sasha before the killer hurt the beagle again.

Or worse.

She hurried along the edge of the platform, past the train cars—beyond the circle of light from the station. Only a sliver of moon shone overheard now, casting a faint glow on her. She glanced down and noticed something on her arm.

Blood?

Was that blood?

If so, it had to be Blake's. Had he been hurt?

He'd assured her that he was okay. Had he been lying? Or hadn't he realized he'd been hit?

Her pace slowed as she considered turning back. But then a shot rang out, the bullet whizzing through the air near Juliette's head. If she turned away now, the killer would shoot her in the back. And she wouldn't be able to help Blake then—if he even needed help.

He'd told her to do her job. And she needed to focus on that now. She needed to stop the killer before he hurt anyone else.

Past the stopped train, she leaped off the train platform to the tracks below. The trainyard was pure dark down there—beyond even the glow of that sliver of moon. She couldn't see anything, but she knew he was down here—somewhere.

As if understanding she needed guidance, Sasha barked again. Juliette let the sound of the beagle's barking lead her farther from the station. She ducked low and peered into the shadows, looking for movement.

Where the hell had they gone? He hadn't had that much of a head start on her. Finally she glimpsed a flash of white and brown as Sasha jumped up and down near a dark train car that sat beside several others on the trainyard. Maybe there had been a stash of drugs somewhere and Sasha had found it.

Or maybe she'd found the killer.

Juliette gripped her weapon tightly as she approached that train car just as Sasha managed to leap up and get inside it. She nearly called her back, but she didn't want to alert the man to her presence yet—if he was inside it.

She wanted to get closer, but she didn't get much nearer before flashes of light emanated from inside the car and gunfire rang out.

Blake pressed his hands against the floor of the train station and tried to push himself up. But his muscles felt strangely weak, and he couldn't summon the strength to push up. So he tried drawing up his knees, too, but pain gripped his side with such intensity that his vision blurred, turning everything black.

He dropped to the ground again, into something wet and sticky. And he realized he was bleeding.

Badly. So badly that there was a pool of blood beneath him. He'd been shot. He hadn't realized it right away. He'd thought just knocking her down had knocked the breath from his lungs. He hadn't realized that the burning feeling inside him was a bullet.

Juliette was going to be so pissed at him. But then he heard more gunfire ringing out—outside the station. And he flinched.

The killer had not given up. He was still trying to take Juliette out. Blake closed his eyes and prayed that Juliette survived—for Pandora's sake.

He didn't want the child to be all alone, and he wasn't sure that he was going to make it. He could feel his blood pumping out—along with his life.

Then consciousness slipped away from him entirely.

Fenwick's heart lurched with dread when he saw the flashing lights on the roof of the vehicle that careened through his gates. He was already opening the front door when Finn rushed up to him.

"What's wrong? What is it?" But he knew: Blake. Blake had been hurt.

"Come with me," Finn told him. Usually the police chief sounded irritated with him. Now he sounded almost gentle as if Fenwick was a child.

He felt like a child as he obediently walked toward the car. A female officer stood next to the open back door.

Was this the woman? The one his son had been following around? As he drew closer, he recognized her as a Gage instead. No. This wasn't Juliette Walsh.

"Mr. Colton," she greeted him, and her brown eyes were warm with sympathy. "I'm sorry…"

His stomach lurched now. *I'm sorry* was what people told you as a condolence.

Was Blake dead?

"Get in," Finn told him. "I'll bring you to the hospital."

*Hospital* didn't reassure Fenwick any. The morgue was in the basement of the hospital. Blake could have been in it, and maybe Finn was bringing him to identify the body.

But if that was the case, he couldn't ask. The words stuck in his throat along with all the raw emotion. He'd been such a fool where his son was concerned—so stubborn and proud. But then, Blake had acted the same way.

They were two of a kind.

Or they had been…

Fenwick ducked his head inside the car and crawled into the back seat. It wasn't empty. A little girl sat buckled into a booster chair. She blinked sleepy eyes at him.

Green eyes. Like his son's.

Would he see his son again?

Finn slid into the driver's seat while the woman went around the car to squeeze in on the other side of the booster chair.

Fenwick wanted to ask what was going on, what had

happened. But all he could do was stare at the child. She smiled shyly at him, and a deep dimple creased her left cheek.

Blake was right.

There was no need for a paternity test. The child was clearly his. She was beautiful.

"Hi, sweetheart," he murmured. He was a grandfather. He had a granddaughter.

The thought humbled and terrified him at the same time. He'd failed miserably as a father. Could he do a better job now? As a grandparent?

Some of his friends claimed that their grandkids had given them a second chance to do it right now. Others just enjoyed spoiling them.

"Are you going to see my mommy and daddy too?" she asked him.

He glanced across her at the Gage woman. Was it safe for the girl to be out? Wasn't the child supposed to be in some kind of protective custody?

"Yes," he replied. "I am."

"My name is Pandora," she introduced herself.

She looked to be barely more than a toddler, but she acted so old for her age, so mature. Apparently her mother had done a respectable job as a single parent. Maybe he'd misjudged the young policewoman.

"What's your name?" she asked him.

His heart warmed his chest, chasing away some of the chill over worrying about Blake. "Grandfather," he replied, his voice gruff with emotion. The word was nearly too big for him, so it was certainly too big for her. He amended, "Grandpa. I'm your grandpa."

"Mommy said Grandpa died a long time ago," she replied, her green eyes narrowed with suspicion.

"She must have been talking about her daddy," he said. "I'm your daddy's daddy."

She nodded. "Daddy got hurt." She glanced at the woman next to her. "That's what Elle said."

He stared over her head at Officer Gage, wondering what the hell she'd been thinking to tell her that. Despite how mature she acted, the little girl was still just a child. A child who'd witnessed a murder already, though. Maybe the policewoman had thought it better to prepare than to shield her.

"He got hurt saving Mommy."

"So Mommy's all right?" he asked. He couldn't imagine if the child were to lose both her parents. Would he be responsible for her then?

She nodded. "She caught the bad guy. He can't hurt nobody else no more."

But before Officer Walsh had caught him, he had hurt somebody. He'd hurt Blake.

How badly?

Finn kept the lights flashing and the sirens blaring the entire way to the hospital—as if he was worried that they might not get there in time.

How badly had Blake been hurt?

Fenwick couldn't ask. And not just because of the little girl being present. He couldn't ask because he wasn't sure he wanted to know yet.

But they arrived at the hospital within minutes of leaving his estate. Finn opened his door for him. When Fenwick stepped out, his legs shook beneath him, and the younger man had to grab his arm to steady him. Fenwick wasn't sure he would be able to handle it if Blake was gone—if he never had the chance to repair their relationship.

Elle Gage had taken the little girl from her booster chair and carried her. But Pandora wriggled free of the policewoman. Then she reached out and grasped Fenwick's hand with her small one. It was surprisingly strong, though. She held on to him tightly as they walked into the hospital.

For her sake and his, he hoped Blake was all right.

# Chapter 25

Juliette heard the automatic doors swish open to the hospital lobby. It was a small hospital, but it still could have been anyone arriving. She was looking for Pandora, though. She'd asked Elle to bring her down because she hadn't wanted to spend another minute apart from her.

And it was safe now. The killer was in one of the operating rooms. Juliette had put another bullet in his shoulder while Sasha had put quite a gash in his arm. If her partner hadn't latched onto him, the guy might have shot Juliette like he had Blake.

Thanks to Sasha and Blake, she was uninjured, though, while Blake was having surgery in another one of the operating rooms. She'd had Elle warn Pandora that her daddy was hurt because she didn't want the little girl to be surprised when she saw him. And she had to see him…just like Juliette had to see him.

She had to tell him she loved him—that she would go with him anywhere if he really didn't think he could stay in Red Ridge. She had been crazy to turn down his offer. She knew now that she would take whatever he could give her—even if that wasn't his love.

When she'd returned to the train station and had found him lying on the floor in that pool of blood…

She shuddered at the memory. One of the bodyguards had been on the ground next to him, staunching the blood with a shirt pressed to the wound. Hopefully Blake hadn't lost too much blood. Hopefully he would be fine…

He had to be fine.

"Mommy!" a little voice called out.

She turned to see Pandora walking into the waiting room. But she was not alone. She held the hand of a familiar, older man. Blake's father.

"This is my grandpa," Pandora told her as if making introductions at one of her tea parties.

Juliette nodded. She had no idea what to say to the man. *Sorry I got your son shot* didn't seem appropriate— at least not in front of her daughter—even though it was an accurate account of what had happened.

Pandora saved her from having to say anything when she tugged on Fenwick Colton's hand until he looked down at her. "Mommy says Daddy is a prince," she told him. "So that makes you a king."

A chuckle slipped out of him. "I'm hardly a king, sweetheart."

Since he was the mayor, some people referred to him as the king of Red Ridge. But that was probably because he tried to rule it like a dictator.

He squeezed the little girl's hand and told her, "But yes, your daddy is a prince—a prince among men."

"A hero," Juliette told him. "He saved my life."

"How is he?" Fenwick asked her.

"The doctor should be out here soon," she said. "He'll tell you." He wouldn't talk to her. She wasn't next of kin. She was nothing to Blake but his baby mama.

The waiting room doors swished opened again, and four women rushed inside—Blake's sisters. They hurried over to their father but stopped short when they saw Pandora holding on to his hand. He picked up the child and told her, "These are your aunties."

"Auntie Layla." He pointed toward the blonde whose hair was cut in a face-framing bob.

"Auntie Bea." This blonde's hair was longer and wavy. She was clearly stunned at her new title, though, her mouth falling open in shock.

"Auntie Patience," Fenwick continued.

The dark-haired vet smiled at the little girl.

"And Auntie Gemma," he said.

The chestnut-haired woman stared at Pandora, her dark eyes wide and filled with horror. She was clearly not a fan of children.

But Pandora was a fan of beauty. She stared at the woman in awe and almost reverently whispered, "You are so pretty. You must be a princess."

Layla and Patience laughed. And Patience said, "She guessed that right."

Gemma smiled back at the little girl. "Well, aren't you a sweetie?"

Fenwick tightened his arm around the child. "Isn't she? She's amazing."

Patience walked over to Juliette and whispered, "Guess he doesn't need that paternity test after all."

So that really had been his father pushing for that, not Blake. Blake had never questioned Pandora's paternity—except the first moment he'd seen her.

He'd known before he'd ever asked, though. He'd known the minute he saw her.

"Mommy, we got a big family now for tea parties," Pandora said. "It's not just you and me anymore."

Her face flushed with embarrassment. While Fenwick Colton had accepted his granddaughter, she doubted he would accept Juliette—especially since it was her fault that his son had gotten shot.

Patience squeezed her arm. "She's right…"

But Juliette shook her head. "She's young." And too naive to understand how the real world worked. Cinderella never wound up with Prince Charming in Juliette's world—in Red Ridge.

The waiting room doors opened again, but these were the ones from the employee part of the hospital. A surgeon stepped through them. Was this Blake's doctor Or the killer's?

Juliette didn't care how the man she'd shot was doing. She cared only about Blake.

"Family of Blake Colton?" he called out.

Juliette gasped. And the color drained from the face of every one of Blake's family members—even his dad.

It didn't sound good—not for the doctor to call out like that, like he was making a notification.

Juliette had had to do that a couple of times when she and Sasha had found some teenagers who died of a drug overdose. She'd felt so horribly for them. It had been the worst feeling of her life until her daughter had been threatened and then Blake had been shot.

His dad turned and handed Pandora to Juliette before heading toward the doctor. But Patience took the child from her arms and handed her to Elle. Then she grabbed Juliette's hand and tugged her along behind her father.

"You're family now," Patience said.

But she wasn't.

Fenwick's throat visibly moved as if he was choking down fear. "How—how is he, Doctor?" he asked.

"He lost quite a bit of blood from the wound, but all his organs were missed. Except for some tissue damage, which should heal quickly because he's young and healthy, he's going to be just fine."

There was a sudden expulsion of air, as if everyone had released the breath he or she had been holding.

Fenwick reached out a shaky hand and grabbed the doctor's. He pumped it in a hearty handshake. "Thank you. Thank you! When can I see him?"

"He's in recovery now. I can take you."

Fenwick started after the doctor, but Patience called him back. "Dad. You should let Juliette go."

She shook her head. "No. No. I wouldn't...his father should go."

Pandora must have wriggled down from Elle's arms

because she was pulling on Juliette's hand. "Is Daddy okay? Is Daddy okay?"

Juliette nodded and smiled. "He's just fine."

And with the killer caught, he would stay that way. He wouldn't have to put himself in danger to protect her anymore. She watched Fenwick walk off with the doctor, and she longed to go with him.

While she believed the doctor that Blake would be fine, she wanted to see for herself that he was. Hell, she just wanted to see him. That wasn't all she wanted to do, though. She wanted to touch him and hold him and kiss him and tell him that she loved him.

That she had always loved him.

And she didn't care if she made a fool of herself.


Finn had not gone inside the hospital with the others. He'd stopped to talk to the officers who'd arrived from the crime scene at the train station.

"Did you find out who he is?" he asked Carson Gage.

The detective shook his head. "Still haven't ID'd him. We took prints from the train car he was in when Walsh shot him, but Katie didn't get a hit yet."

Their tech was the best. If his prints were in the system, Katie would find them. But if he was as good as he seemed to be, maybe he'd never been caught before.

"I saw him," Dante Mancuso said as he joined them.

Finn had sent him in at the last moment—when he'd started thinking about how easily that kid had given up the information to Juliette. Too easily...

But by the time reinforcements had shown up, it

would have been too late—had Blake not jumped in front of that bullet and taken it for Juliette.

"You saw him at the scene?" Finn asked, not understanding what Mancuso meant.

"I saw him before going in and out of the Larson twins' real estate office," Mancuso said.

"Really?" he asked, as excitement coursed through him. Maybe this was it—the break he needed to finally bring down the twins.

Dante nodded. "Sure of it."

Carson sighed and cautioned them, "That alone doesn't prove a thing. He could have been buying or renting property through them."

Finn could guess what kind of property. He'd arrived at the hospital worried only about one man surviving his gunshot wound. Now he wanted the killer to survive, as well—so they could get him to talk. He was facing so many charges, including murder, that he might be convinced to turn over evidence against the Larsons in exchange for a deal.

Finn would call the district attorney—right after he'd checked on his cousin.

Blake must have still been unconscious. That was the only excuse for what he was seeing—his father weeping beside his bed. Tears streaked down the man's suddenly old-looking face while his shoulders shook with sobs.

He reached out and tried to pat his head. "It's okay..." he murmured weakly. "I'm alive..."

His father pressed a hand to his face, as if trying to hide his tears now. But it was too late. Blake had seen them. There was a time that he wouldn't have believed his father cared if he was alive or dead. Fenwick had certainly never called and checked on him after Blake had left Red Ridge.

His dad drew in a deep, shuddering breath and straightened his shoulders. "I—I know that…" His shoulders slumped again, and his voice cracked when he continued, "I just came so close to losing you forever."

"I'm fine," Blake assured him. At least, he hoped he was. He still felt so damn weak like he had when he hadn't been able to get up from the floor of the train station. But at least his side wasn't burning like it had been. It was mercifully numb now.

"That's what the doctor says," his father confirmed. "But I can't get over how close a call you had…"

Blake didn't care about himself right now, though. He remembered the gunshots he'd heard right before he'd lost consciousness. "Juliette," he said. "Is she okay?"

"Pandora's mother?" His father nodded. "Yes, she's fine. She and my granddaughter are in the waiting room."

"And Sasha?" he asked—knowing that like him, the beagle would probably have taken a bullet for Juliette gladly.

His father's brow furrowed. "Sasha? Who's that? Is Pandora a twin?"

Blake chuckled. "Sasha is Juliette's partner. She helped me warn her. She started growling and barking. She saw him before Juliette did."

"Sasha's a dog?"

Blake nodded. "She's very protective of Juliette."

"Patience didn't have to go in to work on her, so I assume she's fine."

If the dog had been hurt, Patience would have been taking care of her.

He sighed. "Good. That's good…" He focused on his dad again. "Pandora is here?"

"Yes." His father smiled. "She's yours."

Blake smiled with pride in his little girl. But he couldn't resist reminding his father, "I told you I didn't need a test to prove it."

"I didn't know if you could trust that woman," Fenwick said.

Blake hadn't known, either. But now he'd realized that he could. That night, nearly five years ago, he'd given her every reason to think he wouldn't want to know he had a child. He'd been so adamant about never being a father or a husband. Now he'd changed his mind about both.

"I can trust her," Blake said. "That's why I'm going to marry her."

Fenwick shook his head. "No way! No way in hell will you propose to her!"

"Damn it, Dad!" Blake yelled as his strength suddenly surged back with his fury. "Don't you dare say she's not good enough for a Colton. She's too good for a Colton. She's too good for me. After her dad died, she took care of her sick mother. When I met her, she was working two jobs to pay off the medical bills and put herself through school. She's proud and smart and brave…"

And incredibly independent. Would he ever convince her to marry him?

"You fool," his father said. "I'm not denying any of that. She must be pretty amazing to have raised that child alone like she has and done such a damn good job."

"Then what's the problem?" Blake asked. And his head began to pound with confusion. Maybe he'd lost too much blood. While there was an IV pumping something into his arm, he didn't feel like himself yet. That spate of anger had zapped what little strength he'd rallied.

"You can't propose because proposing gets a guy killed in this damn town!" his father exclaimed. "I've nearly lost you too many times to let you risk your life again."

"He's right," Juliette said as she stepped into the room with his father.

Fenwick smiled with approval at her.

"You can't propose to me," she said.

But was she saying that because of the Groom Killer or because she didn't love him?

## Chapter 26

Fear coursed through Juliette when Blake slumped over and passed out cold. She rushed toward the bed and felt his neck for a pulse. It was there beneath her fingertips—weak but steady. None of the machines attached to him were going off, so his vitals must have been fine. She breathed a sigh of relief.

"Is he okay?" Fenwick asked, his voice cracking with his fear.

She nodded. "I think he just overdid it."

"*I* overdid it," Fenwick said. "I never know how to talk to him. We always wind up fighting instead."

Juliette had thought he was the last person for whom she would have ever felt sorry—until now. She could feel his pain and frustration. She squeezed his arm.

"You love him," she said. "That's all that matters to him."

Tears glistened in the older man's eyes. "I haven't always shown it, have I?"

She shook her head.

"To any of my kids," Fenwick continued with his self-recrimination.

"It's not too late," Juliette said.

He stared down at his son lying so still in the hospital bed. "It almost was."

"He's going to be fine," she assured him. But she was trying to convince herself of that, too. He was so pale.

"He won't be if he tries to marry you."

She nodded. "I know."

"That's the only reason I said what I did," he continued. "He's right. You're probably too good for a Colton."

She glanced down at Blake again. "Not this Colton…"

Blake was such a good man. A prince. A hero.

His lashes fluttered, and his lids began to flicker as if he was trying to open his eyes.

"I'm going to leave before he wakes up," Fenwick said. "I don't want to upset him again."

"I'll go, too," she said.

But Fenwick squeezed her shoulder. "Stay. He wants to see you."

He wanted to marry her. Had he really said that? Had he said all those wonderful things about her that she'd overheard? Or had her ears been playing tricks on her?

They were ringing a little yet from all the gunfire.

It had echoed inside that empty train car where Sasha had tracked the killer.

"His sisters should come see him," Juliette said. When a nurse had told them that he could have two visitors, all of Fenwick's daughters had urged her to go back to join their father.

She wasn't certain if that was because they'd seen how upset she was or because they hadn't wanted to be in the same room with their father and Blake.

"His daughter should come visit him," Fenwick said. "I'll go get her." He rushed off as if eager to see the little girl again.

"He's going to spoil her," Blake murmured.

Juliette turned back to the bed to find that his eyes were open now, and he was staring at her.

"Are you okay?" she asked.

He sighed. "No…"

"I'll get a doctor," she said, but when she turned to leave, he grabbed her hand. His grasp was surprisingly strong. He was already getting better.

The tightness that had been in her chest since she'd realized he'd been shot eased somewhat. He was really going to be all right.

"The only reason I'm not fine is because you turned down my proposal," he said.

"I didn't turn it down," she said. "I just told you that you couldn't propose."

His green eyes narrowed with irritation. "Same thing…"

"No," she corrected him. "And I'm not saying no. I'm saying not yet. Not until the Groom Killer is caught."

His eyes brightened, and a smile curved his lips. "So you will marry me?"

"I love you," she replied. "I should have told you sooner, but I was trying to protect you."

"You got mad at me for trying to protect you," he reminded her.

"Are you mad at me?" she asked.

He shook his head. "I was at first—for keeping Pandora a secret. But I couldn't stay mad."

"You should have," she said. "You should be furious with me over that. I don't know how you will ever forgive me." She wasn't sure that she could ever forgive herself for the years together that she'd stolen from the people she loved the most in the world.

He reached out with his other hand and slid his fingertips along her jaw. "I gave you every reason to think that I wouldn't ever want to be a father. So I understand."

She released a deep and ragged sigh. She'd worried for so long that he would never forgive her. But he already had.

"You are amazing," she murmured. "Thank you for saving my life."

"Told you that you needed me," he said. But he chuckled self-deprecatingly. "Did you get him?"

She nodded.

And his breath shuddered out in a ragged sigh of relief. "Thank God. Thank you. You really are a wonderful officer. I won't ever suggest you leave your job again."

She smiled teasingly and asked, "Until I'm in a danger again?"

His skin paled again as if that thought hadn't occurred to him. But then he drew in a deep breath and shook his head. "Not even then. I understand how much it means to you."

"You mean more," she told him. "You and Pandora. Now that she's safe, I could leave Red Ridge…" She would feel bad leaving before the Groom Killer was caught. But Blake was more important than anything but their daughter.

He shook his head again. "No. Neither of us is leaving. I'm going to move my headquarters to Red Ridge. I'm staying here. I'm staying—" he swallowed as if choking on emotion before continuing "—home."

"You didn't consider it that five years ago," she reminded him. As well as making love that whole night, they'd talked, too; he'd shared so much of himself with her.

"It wasn't then. But when I came back and found you and Pandora…" He swallowed hard again.

She reached for the cup of ice chips a nurse must have left next to his bed. But when she held out the spoon, he waved it off.

"You and Pandora made Red Ridge home for me," he said. "And I do want you to marry me."

"Why?" she asked. While she'd professed her love, he'd made no declarations of his own.

"Because I love you," he said. "I think I've loved you since that night when we conceived Pandora."

"That was a magical night," she agreed. "I felt like Cinderella. And you were my Prince Charming."

"Prince Charming gets Cinderella in the end," he reminded her.

"This is no fairy tale," she said. She'd stopped believing in happily-ever-afters long ago—when she'd lost her mom. But then she remembered her saying that everything had happened for a reason.

That reason wasn't just Pandora now. Blake was that reason, too.

"We don't have to make it official," he said. "I just need to know that you will marry me. I love you so much…"

She loved him too much to tell him yes. She loved him too much to risk losing him again.

Blake held his breath, waiting for her answer. She just shook her head. And his heart broke.

But she looked like hers was breaking, too, as tears filled her eyes. "I can't," she said. "I can't put you in danger ever again."

"You can protect me," he said. "It's your turn, after all."

Her lips curved into a smile. "Really?"

"I've spent the past few weeks protecting you from this park killer guy…" He sighed wearily. "So it's your turn. You can protect me from this Groom Killer. You're a damn good cop, Juliette. I trust you to keep me safe."

"Yes," she said.

"Yes, you'll protect me? Or yes, you'll marry me?" he eagerly asked.

"Daddy's gonna marry Mommy!" a high voice exclaimed.

"Shh…" Grandpa cautioned his granddaughter as he carried the little girl into the room. "We're going to keep that a secret for a while—just between all of us."

Juliette nodded in agreement. "That's the only way I will say yes, if we keep it a secret."

Blake really didn't want any more secrets between them. But since this was one they were agreeing to keep together, he was fine with it. Hell, he was fine with anything as long as Juliette would agree to marry him.

"I would get down on one knee," he said. "But I wouldn't be sure I could get back up again. So I'm just going to ask you…" He trailed off, waiting for someone to interrupt him.

But she didn't stop him this time, and surprisingly enough, neither did his father.

So he continued, "Juliette Walsh, will you be my Cinderella bride? My wife? My partner? My soul mate?"

She nodded and nodded and nodded. "Yes, yes, I will."

Pandora clapped her hands together in glee. "Yay. Now Daddy needs to give Mommy a ring." And she jerked the candy ring pop from her finger and held it out to him.

Blake exchanged a glance with Juliette. "I told you he was going to spoil her." His father must have been the one who'd bought her the candy. And she must have been the reason that his father had not tried to stop him from proposing—because he didn't want to disappoint her.

And if his father could change that much just since meeting his granddaughter, Blake had no concerns about the kind of father he would be. He would do everything within his power to never disappoint her, either.

He took the ring pop from his daughter's sticky fingers and held out his other hand for Juliette's. She placed it in his palm and he slid the plastic ring over her knuckle. The *diamond* was a half-licked glob of blue candy. But she stared down at it like it was real, her blue eyes welling with tears.

"Isn't it pretty, Mommy?" the little girl mused. "It matches your eyes."

Blake grinned. That it did…

As soon as he was out of the hospital, he would get her something better—something that would last forever—just like their love.

Fenwick Colton had never been as determined as he was now to make sure a wedding took place as soon as possible in Red Ridge. And it wasn't Layla's wedding that he was anxious to have happen.

He wanted his son to marry the woman he loved; he wanted to watch that adorable little girl of Blake's walk down the aisle swinging a basket of flowers. Just the thought of it—of how pretty she would be as flower girl in one of the pretty dresses from Bea's bridal shop—had him blinking back the tears stinging his eyes and burning in his nose.

He had never been as damn emotional as he was now—except maybe when he'd lost his first wife. But he'd nearly lost his son. Again. He'd lost him five years ago when Blake had left the country.

But tonight he'd nearly lost him for good—for dead. And if word got out of Blake's recent engagement, Fenwick could still lose his son—to that psychotic Groom Killer.

Police chief Finn Colton couldn't let that happen.

"What the hell are you doing to find Demi Colton?"

he demanded when he cornered the chief in the waiting room. He wanted that crazy daughter of his trashy cousin's behind bars with the killer who'd tried to hurt his granddaughter and her mother.

"Like I told you before, I'm not sure that Demi is actually the killer," Finn said, and he sounded tired. With the dark circles around his eyes, he looked tired, too.

The guy needed to get more sleep.

But Fenwick hadn't been sleeping himself—not since these killings started and Hamlin Harrington ended his engagement to Layla. Fenwick had been worried about losing his business. But now he knew that was the least of his concerns.

He was worried about his family, and with Pandora and Juliette, that family had just gotten bigger. So he had more to worry about.

"You don't know where she is, so you can't know that she's not in Red Ridge. You need to assign some officers the sole responsibility of finding her."

Finn grimaced.

Fenwick knew that he was telling the man how to do his job. But apparently someone had to, or this damn Groom Killer would never get caught. And since he was mayor, Finn pretty much worked for him, anyway.

"I already assigned two officers to find her," Finn said begrudgingly.

"What? Coltons or Gages?" he asked with a derisive snort. He wouldn't trust either of them to bring her back. The Coltons might let her go and the Gages might make sure she was never found.

"Michaela Clarke and Liam McTiernan," Finn replied. "They're checking all the motels and short-term leasing places across Black Hills County."

Fenwick nodded. "Good. That's good."

They would find her. They had to. Fenwick was pretty sure his son's wasn't the only secret engagement in Red Ridge. There were a lot of other couples who wanted to get married.

After seeing the love between Blake and Juliette, he felt a little uneasy about Layla marrying Hamlin. She obviously didn't feel about him the way that Blake felt about Juliette. But that was just because she was even more like Fenwick than Blake was. She was all business.

Blake was a family man now.

And Fenwick couldn't be happier or prouder of his son. He just wanted to make sure he stayed alive to marry the woman he loved. But he and Juliette had kept each other alive while one killer was after them and their daughter. He believed they would do it now, as well, because they had too much to live for—they had their family.

\* \* \* \* \*

# COMING SOON!

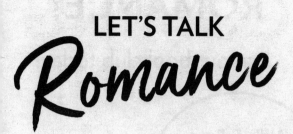

# LET'S TALK
## Romance

For exclusive extracts, competitions
and special offers, find us online:

**f** facebook.com/millsandboon

**⊙** @millsandboonuk

**🐦** @millsandboon

Or get in touch on 0844 844 1351*

For all the latest titles coming soon, visit
millsandboon.co.uk/nextmonth